HEART RAIDER

SOPHIA KNIGHTLY

COPYRIGHT

sophiaknightly@gmail.com
http://www.sophiaknightly.net/
https://twitter.com/SophiaKnightly
Sign up for Sophia's Books News & Giveaways at:
http://sophiaknightly.net/newsletter-sign-up.html
https://www.facebook.com/Sophia-Knightly

NICK AND VERONIQUE - HEART RAIDER

A private island. Scorching summer. Danger lurks...

After a raging media storm nearly destroys him, financial whiz Nick Cameron finds himself isolated and laying low on a barrier island off the Florida coast, far away from the reporters and scandals.

But when Ronnie Whitcomb shows up on the reclusive billionaire's doorstep, all grown up and breathtakingly beautiful, he tries to deny his feelings for her. Fate intervenes and a hurricane strands them on the island together and keeping Ronnie at arm's length becomes the biggest challenge of all.

But daredevil TV reporter Ronnie Whitcomb has an agenda of her own that could get her killed. Ronnie knows there's more to Nick than the hot and juicy scandal he's embroiled in, and she is out to expose the real criminal, whether Nick likes it or not. She refuses to sit by while the world slanders the most honorable and decent man she's ever known...and loved.

But Ronnie may have gone too far this time. Will her snooping unleash more danger than she ever imagined?

PROLOGUE

Thirteen-year-old Veronique Whitcomb gazed at the sparkly stars in the clear North Carolina sky and let out a frustrated sigh. Sitting cross-legged in front of the campfire, she swallowed against the lump in her throat and tried to smile. It was the last night she'd spend with her two best friends at sleep away camp and she wished it would never end. Tonight she'd enjoy their company...tomorrow she'd have to face the disaster called home.

"I hate that we're leaving tomorrow," Veronique said, grabbing each girl's hand. "I'm gonna miss you guys." They'd first started coming to camp as little girls and none of them had sisters. Tash and Teddy would always be her Heart Sisters.

"I bet you'll miss Nick even more." Natasha White's blue eyes danced as she tossed her long strawberry blond hair. "You've been trying to get his attention all summer."

"I have not, Tash," Veronique retorted. *God, had she been that obvious?* The first time her eyes had connected with the deep blue eyes of the cutest counselor at Camp Merry Cascades, her heart had done a cartwheel and was never the same.

Theodora Behr clutched her heart dramatically. "Nick is sooo

1

hot. I can't stop dreaming about him." She grinned and nudged Natasha.

"You can't have him, Teddy. I want him too." Natasha pretended to swoon. "Admit you like him, Ronnie. We all do."

"Cut it out, guys." Veronique's chest hitched at the thought of not seeing Nick again, but she rolled her eyes to hide her feelings.

Natasha smiled. "Hey, you don't have to get so defensive."

"Yeah, we're just messing with you. We won't mention him again. No more Nick—I promise," Theodora said, lifting her right hand in a pledge. "I'm gonna miss you too."

"We have to stay in touch after we leave," Natasha said earnestly.

"Pinky swear." Veronique raised her pinky with the bitten-down nail and ragged cuticle.

"I'm in." Theodora linked her suntanned pinky with Veronique's. "I plan to travel the world and marry a hot prince in a foreign land, but I'll always stay in touch."

"Me too." Natasha looped her bejeweled, manicured pinky with theirs. "I'm going to be a famous Broadway actress," she said dreamily. "Of course…if Nick proposed to any of us today, we'd say yes."

"You promised not to mention him again," Veronique reminded her. "Anyway, I'm gonna be too busy reporting impor-tant stuff to think about marriage. I probably won't marry anyone," she added with a touch of cynicism to throw them off.

"Unless it's Nick!" Theodora and Natasha added in unison and collapsed into giggles.

CHAPTER 1

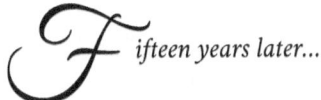 *ifteen years later...*

VERONIQUE SQUELCHED a sharp intake of breath at the dangerous looking man whose wide shoulders filled the doorway. She hadn't expected to find him looking so untamed and ominous on this steamy August morning on Starfish Island, a barrier island off the Gulf Coast of Florida. He looked annoyed too. She couldn't blame him really—she'd stood there ringing the doorbell and pounding on the door until he finally answered.

Nick Cameron's cobalt blue eyes locked on hers, flashing with impatience. Veronique's stomach fluttered nervously as she lifted her chin and stared back, her lips unsteady with the effort to smile. The foreboding glint in Nick's eyes made her knees knock, yet she was not the knee-knocking type—not by a long shot. Veronique Whitcomb, intrepid reporter for Ace News, was not easily frightened. Still...Nick's sheer size and intimidating air gave her pause. She held onto the wooden balustrade and gaped at him. Dark stubble shaded his chiseled jaw. The angles of his face were sharper than she remembered, his cheekbones and jaw taut, his nose a hawkish blade. He was almost unrecognizable, save for the brilliant blue eyes pinning her with an intensity that made her smile falter.

"Ronnie?" Nick's searing gaze raked over her. "What are *you* doing here?"

Her heart lifted. Nick remembered her. Maybe this wouldn't be so hard after all. Maybe the large, scowling man would revert back to the childhood heartthrob she remembered. She'd flown into Miami two days ago from New York and driven across to the west coast of Florida in a rental car, stopping to do some interviews in Fort Myers before crossing over the causeway to Starfish Island. She would have driven *anywhere* to seek him out.

"Never mind. I know why you're here," he said caustically. "You're not getting an interview." He looked behind her, peering from left to right.

"Relax, I came alone," she said, guessing that he was checking to see if there was a camera crew waiting to ambush him.

"You're leaving. Now." His hand on the door, he began to close it in her face.

"Wait a minute!" She stepped up to the door ledge and he took a step backward. "How did you recognize me?"

He looked at her tousled, layered shag with narrowed eyes. "I've seen you on TV a few times—reporting. Your hair's still reddish brown, but you haven't changed much from the thirteen-year-old brat with long pigtails and freckles who raised havoc wherever she went."

"Gee thanks." Why was Nick making her feel like a gauche tomboy when she'd gotten all dolled up in a floral sundress and pretty sandals? She had even put on make-up, for God's sake. She did not look like the ragtag, wild Ronnie he remembered from Camp Merry Cascades years ago.

She drew herself up to her full five foot, five inches. "I *have* changed a lot in fifteen years and you know it."

4

Nick's steely gaze flickered over her flushed face. "Fifteen years or not, I'd recognize your freckles in a heartbeat, especially when you're blushing."

She wished her fair skin didn't turn bright pink under duress. It was one of those things a reporter could do without. Not even the self-tanner she'd applied before coming down from New York could hide her vivid blush.

"Fine welcome after all those years. Aren't you going to invite me in?"

"No." Nick towered above her with tanned, muscular arms folded across his chest and solid legs braced apart. His thick black hair was longer and shaggier than any businessman would ever have. She stared at his well-developed arms and the imposing chest straining his cotton T-shirt. His uncivilized appearance wasn't exactly what you'd expect of a billionaire corporate raider. He looked more like a muscle-rippling wrestler ready to take down his opponent. There wasn't an ounce of fat or flab on him.

Her pulse quickened as she took in every detail. Nick, at twenty when she'd last seen him, had been lean and lanky, but he'd put on at least fifty pounds of roped muscle since. He'd grown a few inches too.

"How did you find me? Nobody knows where I live and I plan to keep it that way," he warned, his voice low and tough.

Veronique lifted her hair up and fanned her neck. "Please let me in and I'll tell you. It's hot out here and these sandals are pinching my feet," she said, shifting from one foot to the other. Why had she even bothered to wear the strappy sandals? Oh yeah, to impress the grouch blocking her entrance.

"Make it brief and then skedaddle. Got it?" Nick opened the door and gestured for her to enter his plantation-style mansion.

Veronique nodded, even though she had no plan to skedaddle. Not when she'd managed to get inside his house. Delighted to pass the threshold of his reclusive digs, she followed him past a high-ceilinged portico and into his living room. As Nick ambled ahead, the play of taut thighs and well-formed butt muscles contracting and relaxing in his low-rise jeans snared her attention.

She forced her gaze away from his jeans and studied her surroundings. A mahogany staircase led to an upstairs loft and other rooms at the back of the house. The living room and dining room were decorated in greige tones, a relaxing combination of gray and beige. Other than basic, minimalist furniture and a few abstract paintings, the house was sparsely decorated.

The living room had a plush, square sectional surrounding an oversized travertine stone coffee table. The dining room, with a long sleek table and six chairs, looked like it was never used. A modern, diamond shaped crystal chandelier hung from a high beam ceiling over the table.

"Aren't you happy to see an old friend?" Ha, she was being delusional. Nick looked ready to throttle her.

His brows knotted over irate eyes. "I wouldn't exactly call you an old friend. More like a little rebel without a cause. I'm surprised they didn't send you home, with all the havoc you raised," he groused. "Especially the last summer you spent there."

Why did he have to mention the worst summer of her life?

"You forget I had famous, rich parents." Damn, this wasn't going as she'd expected...and hoped. She'd wanted him to take notice of the new, grown-up Veronique. "My thirteenth year wasn't exactly a happy one. After Daddy's death and Maman's nervous breakdown, I toughened up real quick."

From that low point in her young life, she had vowed never to feel so vulnerable again. Her father, Brett Whitcomb, a renowned TV news anchorman, had died of a lethal cocktail of drugs and alcohol the summer of her thirteenth year. Her genteel French *maman*, Helene, had always been prone to depression and bouts of paranoia. The more Brett had self-destructed, the worse it had become. She had worshiped her dashing celebrity husband and refused to acknowledge he was an alcoholic and drug addict. When reality finally set in after his death and Helene found out Brett had lost their family fortune in a Ponzi scheme, she spiraled down into a nervous breakdown, leaving behind her frightened, rebellious daughter to cope with the press.

"That was a rough time for you," Nick conceded in a quiet tone. He knew all about her childhood traumas, he'd witnessed them first hand—especially Helene's penchant for high drama and histrionics.

Her thirteenth year was the last time she'd seen Nick—until today. She'd kept tabs on him, rejoicing in his triumphs and success over the years. She met a lot of men in her line of work on a daily basis, but no one had held her interest long enough to build a relationship. Maybe she was "commitment phobic" as Maman often proclaimed gloomily…or maybe no one measured up to Nick. He'd been her hero then and still was, albeit a fallen one. Now that she'd found him, she wasn't about to let things rest until they were set back to right.

Veronique expelled a heavy sigh. "There's no use dredging up bad memories. Mind if I sit down?" she asked, eyeing the living room couch.

"Matter of fact, I do mind."

She paused, gathering courage before he booted her out of there. "I have a proposition for you."

Nick didn't respond. His gaze was so direct, she had to break eye contact and gather her wits. As the seconds ticked by, she realized he wasn't interested.

"Don't you want to know what it is?" She held her breath and waited. He continued to stare at her with a mixture of distrust and skepticism.

"No," he finally said. "But I have a feeling you won't leave until I listen to you. I already told you I'm not giving you an interview. What harebrained scheme are you cooking up now?" he demanded.

She thrust her chin high and narrowed her eyes at him. "I'm no longer a kid and prone to what you rudely refer to as 'hare-brained' schemes. I'm all grown up now, if you hadn't noticed," she stated, throwing her shoulders back and puffing out her chest.

Nick's gaze lowered to her breasts and then back to her face. "I noticed." He shook his head as if to clear it. "Once a hellion, always a hellion."

"I don't remember you being so gruff. You were always nice to me." The Nick she remembered as camp counselor had been on the serious side, but kind and fair.

His upper lip curled. *Damn, how long was he going to make her stand there before him like a delinquent?* With his brawny hands braced on his lean hips and his wide-legged stance he looked like a tough detective interrogating a suspect.

Nick was being so patronizing, she felt like filling him in on the past years of her adult life, the ones filled with awards for investigative journalism and documentaries. But more than likely, he knew all about her recent public shame and how she'd been demoted from foreign correspondent to reporting fluff. She had once been renowned for her daredevil journalism, but given Nick's aversion to the media, it wouldn't be wise to bring it up now. Especially since he too had been publicly shamed in the media, but for vastly different reasons.

Given the way he was glowering at her, she wasn't about to tell him the reason she'd landed on his doorstep was to present Ace News with a prized story. An exclusive interview with Nick Cameron, the notorious, sought-after recluse whose fall from grace had landed on every tabloid would do wonders to revive her flagging career after the fiasco of her last assignment. But that was only part of it; the real reason was to alert him to what she'd found while investigating his recent divorce from tobacco heiress, Elizabeth Remington.

"You still living in London?" he asked abruptly.

His question surprised her. "Nope, I live in New York now."

"Reporting for Ace News?"

She paused. "Yes. I've been reassigned to human interest stories." Her stomach contracted as she said it. The reminder of her recent demotion and near firing still smarted and she'd rather not get into details with him.

Nick cocked his head and quirked a dark brow, the gesture so arrogantly male, it reminded her of Sean Connery when he'd make a sardonic remark in old James Bond movies.

He was making her feel as welcome as a bloodthirsty mosquito. Veronique locked her determined gaze with his as they faced off standing rigidly apart, throwing sparks off each other. Neither spoke until she finally strolled over and plopped down on a duck white canvas sofa.

"Okay, I give. What will it take for you to stop frowning at me?"

"How about you march your little butt out of here?" he asked in a gravelly tone.

He was definitely out to rile her. "How about we make nice instead?" she said with a saucy grin.

Nick lowered his strapping frame into the big armchair across from her, elbows braced on widespread knees. He leaned in nose-to-nose, close enough for her to notice the thick jet lashes framing narrowed blue eyes. Wariness sharpened the hard edges of his jaw line as he watched her intently.

"Tell me. What is so important that you would disrupt my privacy?" he asked, not taking his eyes off her.

Nick was trying to intimidate her, but his closeness was making Veronique weak in the knees and she couldn't help but take a satisfying whiff of him. He smelled wonderful up close—clean and manly and so *delicious*. She exhaled heavily and looked away, willing her body not to react to him, but it wasn't working.

She couldn't tell him his hideaway was the perfect refuge for her while she tried to figure out who had shot at her in the

Miami hotel parking lot, because he'd go ballistic. If no one had located Nick's whereabouts during the six months after he'd disappeared from public scrutiny, they wouldn't find her there either.

The shooting in Miami had happened so fast she hadn't been able to get the license tag number of the drive-by shooter's car. Adding to her frustration, there was no security video of the parking lot. The only evidence of a random shot was her word. She hadn't stuck around long enough to find out where the bullet had landed. The minute she heard the shot, she dove into her car, called 911 and drove to the nearest police station.

She was used to danger, but that random shot had rattled her. It could have been anyone out to get her after the type of investigative reporting she'd done in the past.

Or it could be the case she was currently investigating...

"Answer me," Nick prompted in a gruff voice.

Hunched over like a cagey jungle cat, he didn't look amenable to providing temporary refuge and definitely not an exclusive interview. He grabbed her chin and turned her face to meet his sharp gaze.

An electrifying spark passed from his callused fingertips to her chin. He must have felt it too because he dropped his hand to his knee. Her heart raced and she could feel her pulse throbbing in her neck.

"I, um well..." She was interrupted by a bolt of lightning followed by a loud crack of thunder. The air between them crackled with more electricity than the storm outside. She ran to the large window to get away from him and get ahold of her bearings. "Must be the outer rain bands. Storm's almost here!" she announced breathlessly as the gusting wind swirled outside and the heavy rain pelted the house. "We're in for a downpour."

Nick lumbered forward and joined her at the window. His fingers closed around her elbow. "Time to leave," he said firmly.

"Haven't you been tracking Tropical Storm Abby?" she

asked, disengaging from his grip. "It's sure to be the first hurricane of the season. When was the last time you ventured into town?"

"That's none of your business. Why did you show up here knowing it was heading this way?" His deep voice started off low and increased with each word. While he wasn't exactly yelling, he wasn't whispering either.

Veronique took a step back from Nick's imposing form. "Do you even watch TV?" she blurted out.

"Not if I can help it."

"Why own one if you don't watch it?"

She sucked in a nervous breath. Maybe he didn't know the reason she'd been hauled out of her high-status job as foreign correspondent in Ace TV's London bureau and sent back to the States to report filler stories. She could only hope. It hadn't been her fault that Eric, the fact-checker, had fed her erroneous information on a major political scandal involving a prominent, conservative Senator and a call girl reported to be a spy. When the truth was revealed that she wasn't a spy, but his longtime mistress, Veronique had been demoted and Eric fired.

She missed the excitement of investigative reporting. Not that she minded doing human interest stories, but they weren't as challenging or adrenaline-inducing as breaking a controversial case wide open. She'd had success in cases she'd worked on in the past including exposing a pyramid scheme among top senators, a child porn sting in a Bible belt community, and a heroin operation cover-up in a prestigious private university. The one case she'd tripped up on because of inaccurate fact checking from her trusted co-worker had sidelined her rising career and put her credentials in doubt.

Damn the media and the public for their fickle ways. One day she was at the top of her game and the next, kicked to the curb. Whether Nick realized it or not, she could relate to how he felt.

"I watch it once in a while, but not every day," he said,

bringing her to the present. He frowned. "Quit stalling and get going. I want you outta here before the hurricane hits."

"Pfft. Hurricanes don't scare me," she scoffed. *And you don't either.* "They're pretty exciting. I covered a few and even went surfing just before Hurricane Olga hit. What a rush!"

Nick grabbed the remote control and switched on the news. Five seconds later, when the anchorman said the storm was strengthening into a hurricane, he flicked it off.

"Before you go—and you will soon," he promised curtly. "Tell me how the hell you found me. Nobody knows where I live."

"Well...I wouldn't say *nobody*..." Veronique hesitated.

He crossed his arms over his chest. "I know for damn sure Fred wouldn't give you my address. You must've done major snooping in your step daddy's office to find my whereabouts."

Veronique grimaced. "Who said anything about Fred? He's your lawyer, for God's sake! He would never divulge that information."

"Damn straight he wouldn't." Nick's deep voice rumbled out of his chest like thunder.

Veronique eyed the front door when he stepped closer. It was time to retreat and formulate another plan ASAP.

CHAPTER 2

"*C*'mon, time to fess up." Nick's hands closed over her shoulders and anchored her before him.

Veronique shrugged out of his hold. "I stumbled upon it by accident when Maman insisted that I put a birthday card in Fred's briefcase before he traveled to Europe. That's where I found a letter with your address on it."

If Nick had any inkling of the times she'd tried to wangle information from her stepdad, who happened to be his trusted lawyer, he'd blow a fuse. But ever since she'd read of Nick's public fall from grace, she'd wanted to use her journalistic skills to make things right.

A man of high ideals, Nick had pulled himself up from an impoverished childhood in the backwoods of North Carolina and had never forgotten his roots. Before the dissolution of his partnership with his best friend Zack, and his divorce from his wife, Nick's charity for underprivileged youths, the Cameron Hope Foundation, had flourished with donations, mostly his. He was generous and honest, but he was also tough and strong-minded, which made her wonder why he hadn't stayed after the trial to wreak revenge on his ex-partner and his ex-wife after they'd sullied his good name.

This was Veronique's chance to reveal Nick's side of the story and restore his public image. A blast of optimism energized her at the mere thought of it. Once he was vindicated because of her interview, he would want to rejoin humanity—she could only hope. A smile of anticipation curved on her lips.

"Why are you grinning like that?" Nick's eyes narrowed. "Fred doesn't know you're here, does he?"

From the moment he'd met Nick at Veronique's dad's funeral, Fred Golden had taken a strong interest in the responsible young man. Fred, her stepfather and family's lawyer, had recognized Nick's maturity when he rescued Veronique the night she ran away from camp. He was the only camp counselor who'd gone to her father's funeral.

Veronique had been a tormented little kid grieving the death of her alcoholic, drug addicted celebrity dad and dealing with a mentally unstable mom. Nick had stayed late and made sure she would be okay and Veronique had adored him for it.

Veronique stiffened. "Fred doesn't know my whereabouts and I'd appreciate if you'd keep it that way. I don't want him to know I'm here."

"Why?"

"He and I don't get along much."

Nick slanted a hard look at her. "You better not leak my whereabouts to the public," he cautioned.

"I would never do that!" she said, wounded to the core.

"Good," he grunted.

Nick grasped Veronique's arm and led her to the front door. His grim face showed he meant business, but she didn't want to leave. She wished she could wind her arms around his hard midsection and press her head against his chest as she'd done years ago when he'd comforted her in camp. But she was no longer that teenager and he had become a formidable man. Her stomach gave a little jolt at the strength of her attraction to him. *Chill. Don't let him unhinge you.*

"Please let me spend the night," she pleaded with puppy dog eyes. "I'll leave after the storm."

"No. Go back to Fort Myers while you can. You'll be safer there." He opened the door and nudged her outside.

Veronique felt a whoosh of air lift the back of her dress as the door shut behind her. *Damn him!*

From the doorstep, she glanced at the lush tropical foliage surrounding his plantation style mansion. Wet red bromeliads, soaked birds of paradise plants and damp yellow alamanda flowers glistened with the aftereffects of the heavy rain that had subsided—temporarily. It was typical of those outer rain bands preceding a storm. They came on hard and fast, and then slowed to a fine drizzle until the next one hit.

She pounded on the oak door. "Open up! I need my purse. It's on the couch."

A minute passed before Nick opened the door partially and thrust her shoulder bag at her before shutting it again.

Shaking off his boorish dismissal, Veronique took another look around and was glad she'd photographed the tropical foliage surrounding his house *before* she arrived. If she dared take more pictures, Nick would pitch a fit.

Delighted at being on the tropical island, she breathed in the intoxicating scent of rain and damp earth mingled with fragrant flowers and exotic palms and fruit trees. When she stepped off the veranda, her feet sank into the thick, oozy earth. So much for the flower decorated, dainty sandals she'd splurged on. No matter. She was dying to get out of them anyway—the thin straps were digging into her feet. She took them off and wiggled her toes in the wet, sandy soil as she made her way to the rental car parked beside a coconut palm.

Squish, squish. Her trudge brought back poignant childhood memories of playing barefoot in the beautiful gardens of her parents' estate on the outskirts of Atlanta. She used to love it when it rained and she'd get wet and sloppy, rolling in the leaves and letting the mud seep between her toes and cover her legs so she could arrive at the front door looking like a little piggy just to outrage her meticulously groomed mother.

Oh, Maman, you never did understand my kinship with nature. Growing up with an exquisitely elegant and beautiful mother hadn't been easy. Veronique had had trouble relating to her on every level. As a scrappy kid who much preferred sports to dolls, her ultra-feminine, glamorous mother had always been an enigma to her.

It wasn't until she was an adult that Veronique learned that her mother had met the charismatic TV newsman Brett Whitcomb at a press conference in Paris and allowed him to sweep her off her feet with an impromptu marriage, shocking her pedigreed family in France. Transplanted from Paris to Georgia, Helene tenaciously held on to her cultured upbringing and privileged life.

It was obvious to everyone who saw their mother/daughter dynamic that Helene never dreamt she'd give birth to a daughter who preferred camping to tea parties and jeans to pretty dresses. Veronique had often overheard Maman lamenting that she'd given birth to a scamp instead of a princess. It hadn't really hurt her feelings because Veronique never wanted to sit on the sidelines like a regal princess. She'd much rather be in the thick of things, relishing life with all its bumps and challenges.

A fat raindrop landed on the tip of her nose, signaling the rain was starting up again. She did a fist pump and leaped in the air. Yes! Mother Nature was on her side this time. A looming hurricane would make Nick's naturally protective instincts kick in. She'd leave now because he'd mandated it and she didn't want to antagonize him.

Her toes dug into the soil with renewed energy as she grinned triumphantly. She'd be back—whether Nick liked it or not. He had probably never been in a hurricane if his reaction had been so blasé. His wood-framed, spacious house had a peaked metal roof, horizontal wood siding and side-hinged louvered shutters, with a wide veranda that stretched from one end to the other. The whole structure was surrounded by foliage. The stubborn mule had to realize that electrical power would be the first thing to go after the impact of sixty plus mile winds.

Veronique noticed he hadn't bolted the shutters down yet. Nick wasn't prepared to weather a hurricane—or was he? She'd find out tonight. She could only imagine his reaction when she showed up at his doorstep again. This time, he'd have to let her stay, especially when he saw she brought much-needed supplies. She hoped he would realize he needed her more than she needed him.

If he didn't budge, she'd find a way to make him. Hell, she had survived boot camp for journalists at Camp Fort Benning and had spent two weeks embedded in Afghanistan with U.S. troops.

She danced a little jig and did a high five to the sky. Glancing at the house, she snorted when she caught sight of Nick's looming silhouette as he watched her from the living room window. She had probably confirmed his suspicion that she was still a wild child, but she didn't care, especially after the rude way he'd dismissed her. Nick had sorely underestimated her if he thought he'd seen the last of her.

She intended to ride out the hurricane with him. The tempting thought sent tremors of excitement sprinting through her. A mere hurricane couldn't stop her—and neither could irascible Nick Cameron. She had never backed down from a challenge, and he was a formidable one. But she wouldn't let his bad temper or dismissal of her get in the way. She'd restore his name to its golden luster come hell or high water.

Veronique hadn't earned her childhood nickname "Fearless Ronnie" for nothing.

CHAPTER 3

*G*ood riddance, Nick thought as he watched Ronnie from his living room window. The bewitching stunner was raising her arms and doing a happy dance in the rain. Unlike any lady he knew, she seemed to enjoy her traipse through the mud. At twenty-eight she was still a free-spirited tomboy, though a striking one now underneath the pretty sundress, perfectly pedicured toes, and polished diction. She might have shed her southern drawl for TV work, but she hadn't shed her reckless, impetuous ways.

She couldn't have left soon enough as far as he was concerned. He had only answered the door because he'd recognized her through the peephole as Fred's stepdaughter. The girl had guts, he'd give her that much. She'd met his antagonism with a plucky attitude that hadn't diminished in the past years. As a kid, Ronnie Whitcomb had never seemed to understand rules and limitations, or the meaning of "No." She still didn't. Fiery, sexy and too damned intrusive, she'd managed to get under his thick skin already. The skinny angles of a little girl had blossomed into heart-stopping curves.

Tempting as she was, he just wanted to be left alone. He was tired of corporate corruption and tired of lies—from his colleagues and especially his loved ones. Make that his ex-wife. His emotions had run a gamut of disbelief, rage and contempt as the events of the last year had unfolded. When he realized nothing mattered to him anymore after the trial, he retreated to Starfish Island on Turquoise Bay, a remote inlet that isolated it from the Gulf.

He'd arrived in mid-March when the air was cooler and a bit drier. Whenever he ventured out for walks or swims in the ocean, it was early in the morning or at sundown to avoid the lingering snowbirds and visiting spring break revelers. By April, most of them were gone leaving behind the few local families who lived there year round. He didn't mind the steamy heat and mosquitos that summer brought. The fresh salt air in his lungs and the hot sun beating on his skin felt good. He was here to heal, to bring back meaning to his life—if that was possible.

Each day he spent hiking, fishing or swimming in the gulf brought him closer to some sort of harmony. He knew every inch of the island and often marveled that he had landed in paradise. The ocean's many moods, sometimes placid with still turquoise waters and other times turbulent with white frothy waves, never failed to fascinate him. When he swam in the gulf like a fish, he wouldn't go back to land until his lungs were spent from the vigorous exercise.

He mostly kept to himself, only interacting with others when necessary. In his past corporate life, he used to be friendly and enjoyed meeting people. Now he treasured the quiet solitude so much he couldn't imagine going back to Manhattan. He didn't want to either. He had little human interaction and he planned to keep it that way. For how long he didn't know, but for now it suited him just fine.

He'd paid cash for the sprawling mansion burrowed in deep vegetation. It was a solid structure, built to withstand high winds and rain and surrounded by enough land to be insulated from the public eye. When the garden became a jungle overcome with long grass and weeds, he hired a local gardener and paid him handsomely so he'd respect Nick's privacy. Later, he hired the gardener's daughter as his housekeeper to clean the house and do the marketing.

Nick had felt safe letting only one person know his whereabouts—Fred Golden, his trusted lawyer. Fred was the best. He specialized in handling the wealthiest of clients and one of them had been Brett Whitcomb, Veronique's celebrity father and heir to Whitcomb beauty cosmetics. Fred had watched over Helene like a hawk after Brett's death and eventually married her while Veronique was away at boarding school. She never knew of her mother's pill overdose after her dad's death, and Fred had sheltered her from Helene's demons as best he could.

He had also been Nick's attorney for five years before Nick's public and nasty divorce, and the fall of his financial empire. For the past six months, Fred had provided Nick with the strictest confidentiality and had afforded him with the privacy necessary to dodge the media. He put a plan in motion to fool everyone into thinking that Nick was jet setting around the globe by feeding the media misleading information. He'd also sent postcards written and signed by Nick from key locations to comfort his mom, who worried about her demoralized son.

Demoralized was too weak a word to describe how he felt after being trounced by the events of the past year. Enraged was more like it. After a salacious trial in which his ex-partner and best friend, Zack, was sent to jail for insider trading and Nick narrowly escaped being framed, he found out that his ex-wife Elizabeth had been having a long-term affair with Zack.

He felt like throwing up every time he recalled Elizabeth's last words to him. *"See this bump?"* she'd sneered, pointing to her barely rounded belly. *"I'm having Zack's baby and I want a divorce."*

When the tabloids leaked the demise of New York City's beautiful power couple, Nick distanced himself from the public eye, which led to more juicy speculation. Revolted that he'd always expected the best of others and had blindly trusted Elizabeth and Zack, Nick left town.

Otherwise, he would have killed Zack.

The wisest thing he'd done was to install a punching bag in the gym upstairs and pound it every morning while visualizing Zack's treacherous face. After the first month of boozing, Nick quit cold turkey one alarming morning when he couldn't remember what day it was. Disgusted that he'd almost finished off the destruction that Zack had begun, he dumped the booze out. He'd since gone back to drinking wine once in a while, but not to that kind of excess.

Grueling morning workouts helped him get through the long days, but he still had no desire to be with people again. Not yet and definitely not with someone as tempting as Ronnie. It wouldn't be long before the little pain-in-the-ass snoop began pestering him for an interview. Problem was, Ronnie wasn't little anymore. She was all grown up and affecting his body in ways he didn't care to admit.

She still had a piquant face with mischievous green eyes and a generous mouth prone to wisecracks. Her glossy hair fell in lush layers to her shoulders in vibrant shades of honey, copper, red and chestnut. With a creamy complexion that flushed pink at the slightest provocation, she had a sprinkling of freckles on her snub nose that only added to her wayward appeal.

She sure had filled out nicely too. He'd noted the way her round breasts had pressed against the damp fabric when she'd swayed her arms above her head in that impromptu dance she'd just done. When she'd finally turned to clamber into her car, her wet dress had clung to a slim waist above the saucy swell of her bottom. The corners of Nick's mouth quirked up as he entertained the thought of taking a bite of that luscious Georgia peach.

Heat infused his loins at the thought of making love to her. He clamped his jaw to dispel the image of her pale, slender legs entwined around his hips, welcoming his thrusts with reckless abandon. Ronnie's insatiable thirst for adventure was sure to make her wild in bed.

Nick expelled a deep-throated groan and stepped back from the window when she drove away, determined to put temptation firmly out of sight, out of mind.

VERONIQUE CHECKED her provisions before slamming the back door of her rental car and climbing in again. She never went back to town as Nick had ordered. Instead, she drove to a secluded area near the beach and watched the ocean's waves build as the rain fell. The car windows were opened a crack so water wouldn't come in and she could breathe. Through the narrow opening between the top of the window and the car frame, she relished the smell of salty sea air. Pinpricks of excitement revved her up as she imagined the ocean's magnificence during a hurricane. It would be a sight to behold.

Good thing she'd brought all the necessary hurricane supplies from Miami. She planned to stay at least a few days, hopefully with Nick. When an hour passed, she decided it was time for round two with Mr. Private.

She started the ignition, shifted gears and headed toward the dirt road that led to Nick's place. Holding her cell phone in one hand, she dialed her boss.

"Hey, Tom, just checking in before the storm."

"Where are you?" Tom asked. "There's an order for mandatory evacuation from Fort Myers up to Tampa."

"Is Abby a hurricane yet?"

"Yeah, a category one. It's gaining speed in the Gulf."

"I interviewed some members of a natural disaster survival group called the 'preppers' in Fort Myers. Some interesting characters there," she said, chuckling. "Should make for a good human interest story."

"Don't venture out till it's safe. Helene would not appreciate you risking your life again so soon. She'd be beside herself with worry!"

Veronique stiffened at the mention of her mother. Crusty Tom Leggett was not only her boss, but also a family friend who felt comfortable lecturing her.

"Leave Maman out of this, you grizzly ole bear."

"Dammit, Ronnie, if I hear—"

She waved the phone away from her ear while he blustered. When he finished, she said, "Calm down, I'll be okay. I've lived through many hurricanes."

"Where will you sleep tonight?"

"I'm camping out at a childhood friend's house. I plan on enjoying the fireworks tonight."

"Fireworks?" he asked dubiously.

"Yeah, thunder, lightning, raging winds. All that exciting stuff," she said, not letting on that the real fireworks would be coming from Nick.

"A hurricane is no laughing matter. Be careful," Tom said, sounding more like a father than a boss.

"When have I ever been anything but careful?"

He groaned. "Don't get me started. Your last stunt—"

"Never mind. Gotta go. I'll call you after the storm to check in."

"Hold on. You still haven't told me where you are," he shouted, sounding exasperated.

"Can't hear you," she shouted back. "We have a bad connection. Bye, Tom."

She quickly shut off her cell phone. No sense in wasting a fully charged battery until the phone lines went down, which was bound to happen when Abby hit. Veronique didn't want Tom to know that she'd rooted elusive billionaire Nick Cameron out of his hidey-hole. She'd tell Tom when she was able to deliver a stellar interview with Nick.

No one knew of the convoluted evidence she had uncovered about Nick's ex-wife's dealings that would create a domino effect of destruction if it came to light. She couldn't divulge that to him —or Tom—until her investigation was complete. She planned on telling Nick before Tom, so he could do damage control first.

Hurricane Abby was the first hurricane of the season. Before leaving New York, she'd told Tom that she planned to interview the die-hard locals who never left the west coast, even when threatened by a huge hurricane. Turquoise Bay was rarely hit by hurricanes. The last one to come through was in 2004, when Hurricane Charley rolled ashore. The causeway, which connected the island to the mainland just north of Fort Myers, had sustained minor damage and had been subsequently rein-forced. It took three years to complete and had cost a bundle. She felt confident the new causeway would withstand the incoming storm.

The rain beat harder against her windshield as the car jostled along the narrow road. She'd already changed in the car from her sundress into jeans and a tank top. She'd only worn the sundress so Nick would appreciate her as a woman. But had he even noticed? She had hoped for a glimmer of male appreciation in his keen eyes, but for some lame reason, he still didn't see her as a woman, only as the mischievous tomboy at summer camp.

Veronique heard a loud pop and had to use every driving skill she possessed to control the car as it careened to the left side of the road, almost crashing against a palm tree. When it came to a skidding stop, the vehicle sank to one side, hobbled by a flat tire. She got out and kicked the offending tire. *Damn.* She'd helped her cousin Jeremy change a tire once before, but not in the pouring rain. She felt like screaming with frustration, but didn't indulge in the weakness.

"Don't be a ninny. It's no biggie," she told herself as she heaved a fortifying breath. She buttoned up her bright yellow rain slicker and got out. Pelting rain and strong winds instantly buffeted her

unprotected head as she opened the trunk. The door nearly hit her head as it bobbed up and down in the wind while she pulled out the spare tire along with the necessary tools.

She racked her memory for everything Cousin Jeremy had taught her about changing a tire. She got out the jack and shoved it under the car, pumping hard to raise it from the ground high enough to remove the flat. With two hands gripping the wrench, she grunted and groaned and put every ounce of strength into unscrewing the bolts that held the lug-nuts in place. She ignored the stream of rainwater that poured inside the neckline of her slicker and slid down her spine into the back of her jeans as she squatted beside the tire. When the last bolt finally came free, Veronique rocked back with the force of her efforts and landed with a wet splat in the mud, on the soggy seat of her jeans.

She let out an exasperated snort and shoved her sopping hair out of her eyes, tucking her stray curls behind her ears. Normally, she didn't mind getting wet, but this was ridiculous. Summoning her last reserve of energy, she put the spare on, then forced herself up and put away the flat tire and tools. Her muscles twanged with the effort of keeping balance as the wind and rain swirled around her. She covered the car seat as best she could with the damp towel. It was disheartening to see that her foot quivered when she hit the accelerator. Ignoring it, she clutched the steering wheel and focused on the road ahead.

A bit worse for wear, but triumphant, she was on her way. Dusk was settling in as Veronique pulled up to Nick's. She noticed that the windows had since been shuttered. Well, at least the tyrant wasn't taking the hurricane lightly. She honked the horn and waited a few minutes. When Nick didn't appear, she blared it until she saw the front door swing open.

That got his attention. Wild-eyed with aggravation, he looked like a wicked pirate ready to pounce on her with a vengeance. "What are you doing here?" he roared.

"I brought you stuff," Veronique called out.

When Nick didn't budge from the front door, she lied, "I need help. My foot is hurt." It wasn't *really* a lie. Her right foot had been trembling earlier and she felt gravel grinding into the heel of her foot.

"I have plenty of hurricane supplies," she yelled when he didn't move. "You're going to need this stuff tonight."

The blistering look on Nick's face was priceless before he slammed the front door.

Stunned, Veronique closed her eyes and prayed he would come to his senses and be civil. She got out of the car, adopted an exaggerated limp and hobbled up the path to his front door.

Just before she reached the veranda, Nick darted outside and came toward her in a yellow fisherman's slicker. He snatched the car keys out of her hand and looped one brawny arm around her midsection, hefting her against his hard side. He carted her up the steps in that inglorious way, her feet dangling above the floor.

Within moments, he flung the door open and carefully deposited her in the small foyer. Nick's longish hair grazed his corded neck above the plastic slicker. He smelled good, an appealing mixture of rain and male. Veronique suddenly felt lightheaded. She couldn't blame it on not having eaten lunch today—Nick's heady proximity made desire zip through her like lightning.

He briskly helped her out of her wet slicker and handed her a beach towel. "Dry off. You're dripping on the floor."

Veronique gratefully wrapped herself in the towel and used one corner to absorb the water dripping from her hair so it wouldn't leak on the wooden floor. Mortified, she realized she was shaking. It had to be the lack of food all day.

Nick's large hand curled around her nape as he peered into her eyes. "Hey, you okay?"

Veronique nodded and swallowed hard, determined not to let his tender touch open the floodgates of emotion precariously held in check. All the brashness was knocked out of her at the remembrance of a much younger Nick bandaging her scraped knees after a horse had thrown her, or putting an ice pack on her aching head after a run-in with a soccer ball. Even when she'd driven him crazy, he'd treated her with consideration, just like he'd treated the other kids away from home for the summer.

The most vivid recollection made her eyes well up unexpectedly. She was transported back fifteen years to mid-July at a ranch house in North Carolina where she had huddled in the bushes around midnight, terrified at the police circling the grounds, searching for her.

Nick had been the first to spot her and coax her out. But instead of scolding her because it was the second time she'd tried to run away that summer, he'd patted her back and soothed her while she'd cried her heart out. She had loved being with her friends at camp, but she'd also been desperate to go home, fearing that her dad would self-destruct and die while she was away. Tragically, her fears had been realized when Daddy died that very summer.

Exhausted, hungry, and drenched to the bone, Veronique felt physically and emotionally spent. Nick's gaze met hers with a mixture of exasperation and concern. She wanted to thank him, but she couldn't risk her voice sounding as quivery as she felt—vulnerable and too exposed before his eyes.

"Where are you going?" she asked when he turned and pushed open the front door against a strong gust of wind.

"To unload your stuff before the storm gets worse," he said.

"I'll help."

"No, you're hurt. How bad is it?" he asked, eyeing her foot.

She looked at her foot and twirled it cautiously. "Actually...it feels better now. Must have been gravel in my shoe."

He gave her a baleful look. "Stay here."

"I'd rather help." She felt silly being caught in the lie and didn't like the censure in his scalding eyes.

"No." The rigid set of his jaw convinced her to stay inside while he carried in box after sopping cardboard box of supplies.

In the kitchen, she peeked inside the Sub Zero refrigerator. Surprisingly, it was well stocked with fresh fruit, milk, bread, cheese and cold cuts. The freezer had several neatly stacked frozen meals and a pint of *dulce de leche* ice cream. The state-of-the art kitchen had a stainless steel Jenn-Air six burner gas cooktop and a microwave/convection double oven. The frozen meals had probably been made by a housekeeper, unless he'd taken up cooking. Nick had to have a housekeeper; the place was too tidy and sparkling clean for bachelor's digs unless he was a neat freak and the Nick she remembered wasn't.

Nick returned with the final box and when everything was laid out on the black granite island counter, he turned to her with an incredulous look.

"Who taught you how to prepare for a hurricane?" He gestured toward the batteries, Sterno cans, flashlights, small portable radio, LED lantern, bottled water, canned and dried goods.

"I wasn't a girl scout and summer camp regular for nothing," she retorted with a grin. She pulled a bottle of wine out of her shoulder bag. "Look what I brought for the hurricane party."

"*You* are a hurricane," he stated bluntly. "You look like hell, yet you're grinning with that feisty look in your eyes. I don't know what you're up to, but I aim to find out real soon."

She shrugged. "When Abby hits, you'll be thankful that I saved your hide for the next few days."

"It'll be your hide that needs saving if you don't clear out of here by morning, if it doesn't," he said grimly.

Veronique ignored his rude threat. "Do you realize that within hours we might not have any power? The roads will be blocked by debris and fallen power lines. We might be—"

"We?" he cut in. "I don't like the sound of that, Veronique.

There's nothing I'd like more than to toss you out of here, but you can stay until the storm passes."

She wondered why he was calling her Veronique now. No doubt to get some distance from the past.

"Thanks for letting me stay." He was reluctantly allowing her to stay. Score one for me, she thought, ineffectually hiding her joy. "Since you're in such a generous mood, I'd like to request a hot shower. If you don't mind, kind sir."

"I do mind. Not that it seems to bother you."

"You used to have a beautiful smile. Why don't you smile more often?"

He responded with a snort and abruptly left her in the kitchen. He returned carrying two folded towels and one of his T-shirts.

"Thanks. Which way to the bathroom?" she asked.

"Down the hall to your right."

She lingered beside him, not wanting to go yet.

"Have you eaten dinner?" he asked.

"Nope."

"No wonder you looked lightheaded when I set you down."

"I didn't have time to eat."

"Canned soup and a sandwich will have to do."

She smiled. "Fine with me. I'm not picky."

The air between them was clogged with tension as neither spoke. Veronique was the first to break the silence. "I'm looking forward to a nice, hot shower. I had to change a flat tire on my way back here." She wriggled and gave him an impish grin. "It feels like I have mud and leaves in places a lady shouldn't mention."

"Since when were you ladylike?" The corners of his mouth quirked up sardonically. "You wouldn't be complaining about mud if you'd evacuated like any other sane person."

"Is that an admission of insanity?" When he didn't respond,

she chided, "Don't be ungrateful. I brought the goods, remember?"

"I didn't ask for them, *remember?*" He took her elbow, causing gooseflesh to rise where his callused fingertips touched her skin. He led her down the hall, stopping in front of the bathroom adjacent to the master bedroom. "Here you go. You'll find what you need in there. My housekeeper keeps it well-stocked."

He turned and started walking away.

"You're leaving? I might need my back scrubbed," she said with a coy smile.

"Get going." He opened the door for her and lightly swatted her bottom as she stepped forward.

"Hey, watch it," she said, her hand flying to her bottom.

His mouth twitched. "There's more where that came from," he said dryly.

She rolled her eyes. "Not bloody likely. I know some Tae Kwon Do."

His derisive snort told her what he thought of that as he ambled away.

Veronique entered the black and white marble bathroom and groaned when she saw herself in the wall-to-wall mirror. What a bedraggled mess! No wonder Nick hadn't been tempted to scrub her back…or anything else.

He hadn't been kidding earlier when he'd said she looked like hell. That had been a kind understatement. Black streaks of mascara crisscrossed her pale cheeks. Her freckles stood out in comic relief, the last of her concealing powder and glossy apricot lipstick long gone. Her bangs, usually side swept, were plastered to her forehead and her wet hair was encrusted with leaves and mud thanks to changing the tire in the storm.

She turned away from the mirror and ran her palm across the sleek, white marble counter, marveling at how much Nick's circumstances had changed over the past years. Through hard work and brilliant strategy, he had single-handedly risen from a disadvantaged childhood to a life of wealth and privilege. Despite his fall from grace last year, Nick still indulged his finer tastes. She rummaged through the black mahogany cabinets and delighted in finding the highest quality soaps and shampoo.

She chose a eucalyptus scented body gel and shampoo and stepped onto the wooden floorboard of the glass paneled steam shower. She looked around, entranced by the many choices before her: a hand held showerhead, an eight-jet acupuncture massage shower beside a small cedar bench, and an oversized rainfall ceiling shower. Within seconds, she stood in the soothing mist of a eucalyptus-scented rainfall, feeling as if she were in a tropical rain forest.

Fifteen minutes later, restored and invigorated by the hot shower, Veronique rubbed her squeaky-clean body with a plush towel. Good thing Nick's black T-shirt reached her knees because she'd have to go sans panties and bra until they dried.

She washed her delicate under things by hand, but her outer clothing needed a good washing in a machine. Hopefully, she could get them in the washer and dryer before the power went out. She hung her panties and bra on a towel rack and rolled her jeans and tee in the towel she'd just used to dry off. The other towel was snugly wrapped around her head, turban-style.

Veronique had just taken a deep whiff of Nick's after shave when loud knocks on the door nearly made her drop the bottle. She jumped at the sound of his deep voice.

"Aren't you finished yet? You've been in there a long time," he said.

"Yeah, be right out."

She recapped the bottle and put it back in the cabinet so quickly, the door closed shut with a loud thump.

"Quit snooping," he said gruffly.

She giggled at being caught red-handed, rifling through his personal stuff. Nick knew her too well.

"Hurry up. There's someone here to see you," he added.

Veronique's heartbeat tripped up and her throat constricted. Who could it possibly be? Nobody knew where she was, not even Teddy, her close childhood friend whose family lived in South Beach.

Who would be there to see her in the middle of the storm?

She felt the blood drain from her face as her body tensed, remembering the reason she was there.

CHAPTER 4

"Who's here to see me?" Veronique cautiously opened the door and craned her toweled head from left to right, her eyes apprehensive as she scanned the area.

"Rrruff!"

She jumped when a chocolate Labrador retriever puppy nudged her knee with his wet nose and barked.

"Why are you so jumpy? I just wanted you to meet Baxter," Nick said. Ronnie sure was acting agitated over nothing.

"Baxter?" She pointed to the lab suspiciously. "Is this who you said was waiting to see me?"

"Yeah." Nick watched her struggle to regain her composure as she pet Baxter's fur and cooed over the dog. She'd always been an open book and it galled him to suspect that she was trying to hide something. "Who did you think it was?"

She gave a dismissive shrug. "Never mind. I'm glad you have a dog. He's so cute. Where'd you get him?"

The alluring curve of Veronique's pale, slim thighs snared Nick's attention when she bent forward and scratched Baxter's ears. He noted the sway of her high, round breasts. She probably wasn't wearing a stitch underneath.

Nick looked away and cleared his throat as he hardened with unbidden desire. "He's the gardener's dog. I offered to keep him during the hurricane. He spends a lot of time here anyway."

"Oh, that's nice," she said, giving Baxter a snug, little rubdown. "But why didn't your gardener evacuate and take his dog? Does he live on the island?"

"Yes, there's a group of workers who live in a small house on the grounds of a large estate on the northern tip. They live there in exchange for taking care of the house and gardens while the owners are up north. They only come down in February and March."

"Sounds like a good arrangement all around." She straightened and tugged at the T-shirt's hem, making a production of smoothing it over the backs of her bare thighs as she sauntered by.

Nick's gaze gravitated to the cheeky sway of her bottom. From the way it jiggled slightly, he was certain she was bare there too. Hot lust swelled in his veins, thick and opulent.

"I'm starving," she said over her shoulder. "Can we eat now?"

"Sure," he said and forced his gaze away from the tempting sight.

"Looks delish." She smiled as he served her a bowl of minestrone soup and a ham and cheese sandwich. "Let's have some of that wine I brought."

Nick filled two wine glasses with Malbec and joined her at the kitchen table.

"Thanks." She clinked his glass with hers. "Here's to old times, Nick."

He wondered at the vast relief on her face when she'd found out the visitor was his dog. Just a few minutes ago, she'd looked shocked and then relieved. Now she looked too damned comfortable.

With her face scrubbed clean and her shampooed hair wrapped in a towel, Veronique looked fresh and appealing. Her small pink earlobes drew his attention as he imagined how they'd taste between his lips. His gaze roved over her velvety neck and lower to her nipples where they pebbled against the soft cotton fabric of his T. Another tightening of lust made him adjust his position on the hard chair.

She was going to be trouble.

"How come I didn't meet Baxter earlier?" she asked, drawing attention to her pursed mouth.

"He was in the backyard."

"No wonder I didn't see him. It's an awfully big yard." She motioned toward her bowl. "Aren't you going to join me?"

"I'm not hungry. I ate a while ago."

"That never stopped you before. You used to wolf down every meal or snack that came your way."

Well hell, I was making up for the lack of food during the rest of the year. It was feast and famine during the four years he'd worked as a summer camp counselor. Famine during the school year when his mom could barely feed his little sister and him, and feast at camp when he could eat all the good food the rich little kids turned their noses up at.

Nick's paychecks those summers had gone toward paying for the family groceries. His mom had worked two jobs to make sure he and his sister ate and had a roof over their heads. They'd never gone on food stamps, but they'd also eaten the cheapest ground beef in every way imaginable. He had vowed early on never to eat ground beef or peanut butter again.

"I never saw anyone eat so much," Veronique continued.

Nick snorted. "Yeah, unlike you little rich girls who thought the camp food beneath you."

"I did not. I wasn't eating because I thought a hunger strike would get me out of there so I could go home and check on Daddy." She jutted her chin. "When that didn't work, I gave up because I was starving."

He hiked a cynical brow. "How long did it take before you caved—one skipped meal?"

"No. Two or three," she admitted with a wry smile.

"You girls didn't know how good you had it. Even if I was working 24/7, it was a luxury to do camp activities I'd always craved growing up."

"Such as?"

"Horseback riding, canoeing, hiking, swimming, those sorts of thing. Living the life—if only for three months a year."

She smiled. "You were a natural athlete. Still are."

"Thanks."

"At the time, you didn't seem to resent us." She leaned her chin on her hand and regarded him with pensive eyes. "Did you?"

"Only when you got me in trouble. Your skinny dipping exploit nearly got me fired from a job I badly needed."

"There's nothing wrong with skinny dipping. Frankly, the fewer clothes I wear the happier I am," she said with a shameless smile. "I'm sure you've done it too."

"It's one of the perks of living in isolation. But a little girl has no business swimming buck-naked in broad daylight, especially when at thirteen you already had a woman's figure."

"I thought everyone had gone horseback riding. How was I to know you were still around?"

"Your socialite mama was pretty scandalized that I had seen her precious little darling in her birthday suit. Luckily, the camp director didn't budge in defense of me."

"I went to bat for you too," she reminded him.

He nodded. "I remember."

"Anyway, all that's in the past. You didn't get fired and you're a success story."

He took a long swig of the wine. The admiration on Veronique's face ate at him like acid. She had an untarnished image of him from her childhood that hadn't been damaged by all the media hoopla. Her loyalty humbled him.

"Hardly," he said. "Let's not forget the past year's debacle."

She shook her head stubbornly. "You're still that successful, self-made man, Nick. What I admire most is your integrity. Nobody can take that away from you unless you let them. I never believed a word of all that crap the media put out there."

"Thanks," he said, touched by her faith in him. Even as a child, she'd been his champion. Especially when she'd stood up to her Mom after the skinny dipping episode and fought for him like a tigress.

"I want to present your side of the story." Veronique's green eyes blazed with zeal. "When people hear you—"

"No. Let's change the subject," he cut in abruptly. He felt badly when her eyes clouded with hurt, but knowing Ronnie, she'd continue to try to wear him down unless he was firm.

She lapsed into silence, a rarity for her. He should have enjoyed the respite, but for some reason he felt like talking tonight—just not about the past year's calamity. He hated to admit it, but Ronnie's lively personality entertained him.

Nick watched her finish the minestrone soup and share her sandwich with Baxter, who gratefully licked her hand after each morsel. At camp, she had always had bits of apple or carrots in her pockets to feed her horse before and after riding it.

When she finished eating, her green eyes sparkled and her cheeks glowed pink with vitality. She looked eager to take on the world as she pushed her chair back and rose from the table.

Nick snagged her wrist and tugged her back down. "Not so fast. I have questions for you," he said, noting how slight her slim wrist felt in his hand.

"Sure, fire away, Nick." With a quizzical lift of her brows, she glanced at his hand circling her wrist.

He released it and asked, "Why were you so spooked earlier?"

"Spooked? When?" Her feigned innocence annoyed him.

"When you thought someone was here to see you," he prompted.

She shrugged. "You surprised me, that's all. Nobody knows I'm here. Who would come all the way out here in the middle of a hurricane just to see little ole me?"

Nick leveled a firm look at her. "I want the truth. All of it."

She drummed her fingernails on the table.

He covered her hand with his to stop the annoying sound. Big mistake, her hand felt incredibly soft and delicate under his, giving him a jolt of pleasure.

"I'm waiting. Are you in some sort of trouble?"

"Heck no!" she said, rolling her eyes.

"Have you made any enemies lately?"

She shifted in the seat, and her round breasts swayed slightly drawing his appreciative gaze. She might look sexy as hell in his T shirt, but he'd have the truth, and he'd have it now.

"Maybe." She nibbled on her lower lip reflectively. "A few, I guess. But in my job, that's inevitable."

"Sounds like you need to be careful, Ronnie. Enemies in your line of work are dangerous."

"Let's not talk about that." Veronique stroked the wineglass stem with her pointer finger and kept her eyes averted. She blithely ignored his concern as she took a sip of wine and said in a light tone, "I'm here to do human interest stories after Hurricane Abby. I had fun interviewing a group in Fort Myers called the 'preppers'."

"The preppers?" He gave her a dubious look. "Do they work in a hospital?"

Veronique chuckled. "Nooo, but I guess it sounds like they do. They're dedicated to being prepared for any emergency, whether it's a natural disaster like a hurricane or an economic one. Some of their members are pretty hard core."

Nick's brows drew together as he regarded her keenly. "What do you mean by that?"

"They own farm animals and grow their own food so they can

have enough provisions for three or four months in case of an emergency. Many are trained in weaponry too."

"How big is the group?"

"It's estimated at about three million throughout the U.S."

"Interesting. Should make a good story."

"Thanks. That's not the only story I want to write." She paused and gave him a hesitant smile. "Actually... I was hoping you'd give me an exclusive interview."

He wanted to wring her neck. "No. I already told you I won't do any interviews," he said in a taut voice. "If it wasn't for the storm, you'd be gone by now."

"Please reconsider." She watched him with earnest eyes. "You've lived life by a strong code of ethics and high ideals. It's not fair the way the press has treated you. I can help clear your name."

"No interview. You're not going to wear me down, damn it. Don't mention it again," he gritted out forcefully.

"Fine, I won't." Veronique's shoulders started to slump, but just as quickly she snapped them back and straightened her spine. She laid a slim hand on his biceps that felt delicate on his arm. Once again, he was struck by the soft silkiness of her skin.

"Thanks for putting me up tonight. It'll give us a chance to catch up after all these years."

She was a fresh one, acting like they were old friends. He couldn't resist having a little fun with her as he said cryptically, "If you knew the history of this house you wouldn't want to stay even one night."

Veronique's eyes sparkled in a lively face awash with curiosity. "What do you mean?"

He took his time scratching Baxter's ears and head before he answered, adding to her eagerness. "A few years back there was a gruesome murder/suicide committed in this mansion. It's said to be haunted by ghosts."

She leaned forward, her face flushed with excitement. Her appetite for details and information was unquenchable. He gave a short bark of laughter. It sounded so rusty he realized he hadn't laughed in a long, long time. Another reason he had to send her packing. Being around Ronnie, one was bound to laugh with the way she lived exuberantly. She had a ready smile and a playful twinkle in her eyes that made him want to pull her in for a long, deep kiss.

Her arched brows knitted as she gave him a puzzled look. "Why did you laugh?"

"You're a nosy little cat," he said, making sure not to say sexy instead of nosy.

She grinned, eyes sparkling. "Not nosy, just interested."

He remained silent, knowing she wouldn't let it go.

"Tell me about the ghosts. When exactly did the murder happen?" she asked.

"'Bout five years ago. Nobody comes around here except my housekeeper and the gardener."

"Really?" Veronique's bright eyes widened. "Do they know about the ghosts?"

"Why so many questions?"

She gave an exasperated sigh. "What's wrong with asking questions? You throw out a story about ghosts and a murder/suicide, and then expect me not to want the facts."

"Some other time." Nick's eyes zeroed in on her. "You were planning on staying here from the beginning, weren't you?"

She blinked. "Why do you say that?"

"While you were in the shower, I moved your car up close to the side of the house and I found your suitcase in the trunk."

"Oh, well…" She had the grace to look sheepish.

"No more tricks and we'll get along while you're here. You can stay until it's safe for you to leave and then it's *adiós*. Got it?"

"Got it," she said amiably. "I'll be gone before you know it."

Right. The little schemer was probably already hatching a plan to stay longer.

"Where did you put my suitcase?" she asked.

"In the first bedroom down the hall, past the bathroom. I'm going to listen to the news now."

"I'll join you as soon as I rinse the dishes."

Nick nodded and headed for the living room on stiff legs. In his mind's eye, he could still see the tempting jiggle of her cute ass beneath his T-shirt and the curve of her bare breasts nestled inside his shirt.

Down, boy, he told himself with a wry shake of his head.

a booming crack of thunder jarred Veronique awake. She rubbed the sleep from her eyes and switched on the lamp beside the bed. Hurricane Abby was finally here.

She usually slept naked, but tonight she had slept in Nick's T-shirt and bikini panties. She ran to peek out the window, but stopped when she remembered it was shuttered. She hefted her purse, which carried her life's essentials and reporter's tools, onto her shoulder, grabbed a flashlight and then inched her way down the corridor in search of Nick's room. Just as she turned a corner, an earsplitting crash stopped her cold—that and the impact of bumping into something solid.

"Oomph!" she said, colliding smack into Nick's bare chest. "What was that noise?"

"I'm not sure. Could be one of the big trees was hit by lightning." Nick steadied her waist. "Are you all right?"

"Yes." It wasn't the hurricane, but Nick's strong hands on her that was making her weak-kneed. She forced steel into her backbone and eased out of his grip. "I'm pretty stoked about the hurricane. It's going to make a great story."

Nick cursed. Obviously, he didn't share her excitement.

"Come on." He grabbed her hand, switched on the hall light and pulled her towards the master suite, with Baxter panting at his heels. When they entered, a crackling bolt of lightning struck, followed by a blast of deafening thunder. The hall light went out and the house was draped in darkness. "Quick, get into the master closet."

Veronique aimed her flashlight at Nick's hard-muscled torso above his faded jeans. Awestruck by the sheer immensity of his strength, she stared at the beautiful lines of his sculpted body.

"Hurry up. We're in for the worst of it." He grabbed a yellow industrial flashlight from the nightstand and tugged her along.

Once inside his closet, Veronique's nostrils were greeted by the scent of cedar walls. She inhaled deeply, thrilled to have a firsthand look at his closet without having to snoop. The cedar-lined room was about eight by ten feet, filled mostly with T-shirts, jeans, and khakis.

"Nice," she murmured as she settled cross-legged on the oak plank floor. Crooning soothing words, she pet Baxter who plopped down beside her. Veronique enjoyed another glimpse of Nick before he switched off his flashlight.

"Turn yours off too," he said. "We need to save the batteries for later."

Veronique complied and listened to the whistling wind and the rain pinging against the metal roof. She wished they could be outside to witness it.

"Thanks for letting me stay," she said, scooting to sit beside Nick, thigh to thigh.

Baxter groaned a few times, settled near them and soon was making little snoring noises.

"I know Baxter ate a lot, but just listen to him. He's sleeping like we drugged him," Veronique said in disbelief. "He's the only dog I've ever known not to freak out over a storm."

"I've never seen a dog sleep through a storm either. He's pretty mellow."

"Could be he's tired after all that playing he did in the rain this afternoon."

Nick nodded, but didn't add to the conversation.

Veronique smiled, imagining what Teddy and Natasha would say if they knew she was holed up in a closet with Nick. The three of them used to sit for hours, giggling and imagining that their favorite, cute counselor had favored one of them with a special smile or some form of attention. Nick had been strong and mature for his age—much more than the other camp counselors. While the others had goofed off at night, he'd been up late reading or studying. He'd always be her Jake Ryan from her favorite teen movie,"Sixteen Candles".

On impulse, she touched Nick's shoulder and kissed his cheek. His jaw tensed beneath her lips. "What was that for?" He sounded gruff at being caught off guard.

"Just wanted to show you how much I appreciate you taking me in. You're the best, Nick," she said, meaning every word. Her cool fingers touched the rigid side of his face.

He clasped her wrist and lowered her hand. "You're playing with fire, Ronnie."

"If you're fire, I want to get burned," she said without hesitation. She'd often been criticized for being too impulsive, but she couldn't hold back. Not now when Nick was seeing her as a woman. This might be her only chance. There was no turning back.

"Sweet talk isn't going to get you that interview," he said edgily.

He thought she was seducing him for an interview? She should have been insulted, but this was Nick, and he'd been burned one too many times by the people he'd trusted. She understood why he would say that.

"It's not sweet talk. I've had a crush on you forever. Wasn't it obvious at summer camp?" she asked, touching his stiff arm.

"No. You were too busy cooking up trouble for me to notice." He sounded surprised.

"After that last summer at camp, I kept up to date on all your achievements over the years, and I couldn't be prouder. I always knew you were a leader and that you'd be a huge success. You are the most decent and hardworking person I know. I meant it when I said you're the best, Nick."

"Come on," he said, sounding skeptical.

"It's true I'm being sincere," she said, edging so close she felt the heat emanating from his powerful body. Nick's sexual energy crackled around them and she wondered if he could hear her wildly galloping heartbeat.

He surprised her by cupping her chin and tilting her face upward. She went still as he held her face in his hands and bent his head to cover her mouth with his. He pressed his warm lips against hers and kissed her slowly, triggering a wave of pleasure so acute, she caught her breath. His tongue teased the seam of her lips until she parted them and he explored the contours of her mouth, his tongue deliberately sliding and stroking against hers, tasting her thoroughly.

Veronique wound her arms around his neck and pulled him closer, welcoming everything—his erotic tongue, his heady taste, the firm pressure of his mouth on hers. Oh God, he smelled divine. His male scent drew her like nothing she'd ever experienced.

She moaned into his mouth as his strong hands lowered from her face and slid down to stroke her sensitized back. She pressed her breasts against his hard chest and they pebbled into tender points as he held her anchored to him.

Heavy, drugging desire formed a delicious pull in her lower belly, pulsing inside her, building a restless ache between her thighs. She yearned for him, wanted him so badly she could barely catch her breath. Her skin was chafed where his shadowy beard had rubbed against and her mouth felt swollen and achy from his hard, hungry kisses. She didn't want to break contact, not even for a second.

She placed a tentative hand on his muscled thigh, and when he shifted positions, her knuckles brushed against his hard erection, but she didn't move her hand. Nick groaned deeply into her mouth and pushed her hand away.

Veronique watched him draw in rough, jagged breaths. His nostrils flared and his breathing was labored as he swore under his breath. Sexual tension emanated from him like a force field and every muscle in her body tensed with longing. She bit her lip to stop from pleading for him to continue. He'd almost lost control, but there was no way Nick was going to let an investigative reporter into his well-guarded life, especially when he didn't trust her. After his ex-wife's deception, he probably didn't trust *any* woman. He'd become a loner, emotionally and physically.

Heat crept up from Veronique's neck, making her cheeks flame. Grateful for the darkness surrounding them, she darted up from the floor, rousing Baxter from his nap. The dog stirred and started to get up.

"Sit, Bax. Sit." Nick patted the dog's rump until he sat back down, panting. "Where are you going?" His hand on Veronique's calf raised a trail of goose bumps on her skin, and she shivered as she slid open the closet door.

She couldn't stay there blushing like a fool. She felt splintered, her feelings laid bare and rejected by a man too distrustful to love again. It was painful to admit, but she understood where he was coming from. She herself was terrified of falling in love. It always led to pain and suffering. She'd seen what it had done to Maman, and many of Veronique's friends were already divorced after only a few years of marriage.

The weighted atmosphere of Nick's frustration and unspoken regret set her nerves on edge. She needed an escape plan and suddenly remembered the half-finished bottle of wine on his kitchen table. She could use a bit of *vino* to compose her tattered emotions.

"There's something missing from our hurricane party," she blurted out and instantly felt stupid for referring to what they'd just shared as a party. What was wrong with her? She was unhinged by his nearness…and his kisses. Hot, carnal kisses that had robbed her of her senses. He wasn't the first guy who'd ever kissed her, but he was the best. So skilled was he that no man would ever measure up.

Veronique dashed toward the kitchen, ignoring his calls to come back. Stumbling down the dark hall, she wished she'd thought of bringing a flashlight. Too late to turn back now. She slowed down and made her way to the kitchen, telling herself all was not lost. They had a whole night together. Nothing could ruin it. She'd somehow get him to relax and then things would resume. One small step at a time, she'd get him to open up.

Bolstered by her plan, she returned and sat beside him, bottle in hand.

"Want some?" she asked, extending the bottle before she took a sip.

He tensed. "Damn it! Don't ever pull a stupid stunt like that again. You could have fallen with the wine bottle and cut yourself." His harsh tone startled her.

"Oh please, nothing happened," she said lightly. "Chill. Finding my way to the kitchen was no big deal. Maneuvering a dark hall is nothing. You forget I've been to Afghanistan."

Nick drew a forceful breath. "I don't give a damn where you've been. It'll be a miracle if I don't put you over my knee before the night is over," he growled, taking the bottle from her hands. "I'd relish it too."

"Brute."

"Brat."

She hated that he was back to treating her like a brat. Veronique wrestled the bottle out of his grip and took a sip straight from the bottleneck. Try all he might, there was no denying that *he* had kissed *her*. Hungry, driving kisses of a man ready to mate. Her body still tingled in intimate places and her heart lifted when she remembered how he'd struggled to stop. He'd looked almost savage when he thrust her away from him.

"No sense in wasting good wine. Have some," she said, extending the bottle.

"Not now." His tone was clipped as he pushed it away.

"Suit yourself," she replied and took another sip.

They lapsed into taut silence, awed by the roiling wrath of Hurricane Abby. The racket of howling winds and loud thunder was magnified by what sounded like a train ricocheting back and forth across railroad tracks on the roof of the house. She inched close to Nick until their thighs touched, but he moved and put distance between them.

A loud rumble followed by falling debris made Veronique grab the flashlight on the floor and turn it on. Astounded, she saw some ceiling plaster had landed directly on top of Nick, covering his hair, face and shoulders in lumpy white powder. His black eyebrows and lashes were comically dusted white as he blinked and sputtered against the plaster covering his lips.

Veronique lost it when she saw the shock on his outraged face. Her laughter agitated Baxter and he jumped around Nick, barking loudly.

"What's so funny?" Nick asked, brushing the snowy particles off his hair and shoulders.

"You should see yourself," she said, waving the flashlight in his face. "You look like the abominable snowman and you've scared the daylights out of poor Baxter."

Nick's scowl softened as he stroked Baxter. "Shh, settle down, Bax."

The pup's barking subsided until another loud rumble sent another coating of plaster in Nick's direction, landing on top of the two of them.

"Shit!" Nick roared, causing Veronique to giggle again.

She took her camera out of her purse and aimed it at him. "Smile," she said and clicked the picture before Nick could object.

He pulled the camera out of her hands and put it up on the top shelf, out of reach.

"I'm sorry. I couldn't resist. You look hilarious covered in white dust," she said, fighting chuckles. "I'll give you a copy." She kissed his jaw, noting how it clenched under her lips. "Come on, Nick. Give me back my camera. I got some great shots of the cove yesterday."

She didn't dare tell him she'd also videotaped his house and the surroundings. When she finally managed to convince him to do an interview, it would make for great visuals to add to his story.

"I won't take any more pictures."

"Damn right you won't. I'll take the wine too," he said, grabbing it from her hand. He set Baxter down and headed toward the door.

Veronique's ringing cell phone caught her attention. She dug inside her purse to locate it.

"Hello?" Bits of static and garbled words met her greeting. "Hello," she repeated.

"Ronnie, it's Natasha." As a favor, Natasha had agreed to stay at her New York studio apartment and cat sit while Veronique was in Florida covering the hurricane.

"Hey, Tash. How's my little Slinky?" Veronique asked, missing her fur baby.

"I'm sorry to call this late, but something horrible has happened," Natasha said, sounding terribly distressed.

An ominous tremor wracked Veronique's suddenly chilled body. "What happened? What's wrong?"

Static broke up and muffled Natasha's response.

"What did you say?" Veronique asked frantically. The receiver went dead in her hand. She jumped to her feet and started pounding Natasha's number on her cell phone, but couldn't get reception.

"There's no signal! Why won't it connect?" She tried again, cursing under her breath.

"Who was that?" Nick asked.

"Natasha White. You remember her from camp, don't you?"

"Yeah, the actress. You still keep in touch?"

"Of course," she said automatically. "We're Heart Sisters."

Nick closed the space between them. He cupped Veronique's chin with his hand and peered into her eyes. "What's wrong? What did she say?"

"She said something terrible has happened, but I don't know what it is. We got disconnected and—"

A high pitched shriek ripped through the night, silencing her next words.

CHAPTER 6

"What was that?" Veronique's heart hammered against her chest as she clutched Nick's arm in a death grip.

Flashlight in hand, he stepped out of the closet. "Stay here while I check."

Grabbing her flashlight, she promptly followed him with Baxter at her heels.

He turned to her. "Hey, I told you to—"

His words were interrupted by a young woman who appeared out of nowhere and flung herself at him. If he hadn't been so large, the impact would have knocked them to the floor. Nick grunted as he steadied her before him.

Baxter's tail wagged vigorously at her arrival. He barked and circled the girl until she acknowledged him.

"Baxie! I'm so glad you're okay," she said, kissing his furry head. That girl was no stranger to him.

Veronique pointed her flashlight at them.

"Thank God, I found you. Where were you?" the girl asked Nick between gasping breaths. When she got a closer look at him, she made the sign of the cross. "*Dios mío*, what happened to you, Señor Nicky? Why are you covered in white powder?"

Señor Nicky? Veronique stared at them open-mouthed. The startled, irate look on Nick's face was priceless. His eyes sparked blue fire and his lips pressed into a grim, thin line. Tension sharpened the chiseled planes of his face.

"Daisy, what the hell are you doing here?" he gritted out. "Why were you screaming like that?"

"A tree crashed through my window and barely missed my head," she said, her black eyes blinking rapidly. "I could have died."

"Does Felipe know you're here?" Nick asked, not offering sympathy. He looked fit to be tied.

"*Sí*, Papi knows." Daisy looked away from Nick's severe gaze and drew in a shaky breath.

"When did you get here?" he demanded.

"Um…this afternoon." She twirled a long lock of hair as she peeked at him from beneath her lashes. "I stayed in the guest-house to help you clean up after the hurricane."

"You shouldn't have done that," he said, his jaw set.

"Why not? I wanted to help." When he didn't respond, Daisy turned her attention to Veronique and pointed. "Who's that?"

Veronique noted the disdain in her voice. She moved the flashlight up and down to get a better look at Daisy. The girl had long dark hair and big doe eyes that gazed at Nick adoringly. She wore a gauzy baby doll nightie that grazed the top of her thighs. Exuding earthy sexuality and a heap of self-confidence, she stood with her hands on her round hips, her back arched and breasts thrust forward.

"I'm Veronique, a childhood friend of Nick's. Who are you?"

"Daisy Martínez. I'm—"

"Daisy is my housekeeper," Nick cut in.

His housekeeper and what else? Veronique lowered her flash-light. She didn't feel like looking at Daisy anymore, especially when it was obvious the girl was enamored with him. The venomous look she had aimed at Veronique proved it. There was no time to dwell on what Daisy felt for "Señor Nicky." Veronique was still reeling from Natasha's phone call and needed to contact her ASAP.

Daisy visibly puffed up with pride. "I cook his meals, wash his clothes and clean his house," she said with a smug smile.

In other words, she was his self-appointed surrogate wife. *What other comforts did she provide?* The girl looked like a teenager, but acted like an experienced woman. There was too much familiarity in Daisy's manner. Veronique didn't like it, not one bit.

"How industrious. That's a lot of work for *such* a young girl," Veronique murmured.

Daisy's chin went up. "I'm not that young."

Nick grabbed each of their arms. "Let's go."

"Where are we going?" Veronique asked, noting his firm grip.

"To the kitchen storage room. It's big enough for three," he said in a taut voice.

"Hold on. Be right back." Veronique dashed into the closet and grabbed her confiscated camera from the shelf. She stuffed it into her shoulder bag before Nick realized she had it.

When she returned to his side, Nick led the way. His body rigid, he moved forward, illuminating the hall with his flashlight. Veronique followed, and Daisy sashayed behind them, with Baxter at her heels.

When they settled inside the pantry storage room, Veronique tried calling Natasha again. After several unsuccessful attempts, she gave up and reached for the battery radio in her purse. They listened to a weatherwoman announce the eye of the storm was approaching. Good, it was halfway over. Unfortunately, the last half of the hurricane would be worse than the first with possible tornadoes predicted.

When her eyes adjusted to the darkness, Veronique noticed they were surrounded by rows of food and provisions. Nick had enough reserves to last for weeks. No wonder he'd been annoyed when she'd shown up with her stash of groceries. She had felt like his savior, but the man never needed saving.

Nobody spoke until Nick unexpectedly asked Daisy, "How is your son?"

Daisy had a son? Was she married too?

"Manolito has a cold, but Mami knows how to take care of him better than I do," Daisy said with a chuckle. "She's been watching him all week." She smiled at him. "Thank you for asking."

All week? What kind of a mom was she? Veronique couldn't figure out Daisy's situation, whether she was married or a single parent, but it was clear her mom helped her out a lot.

They grew silent again and Veronique felt Nick's tension escalating along with Hurricane Abby's wrath. It was rotten timing that Daisy had ruined their intimate moment in the closet. They sat in stiff silence while the girl made a production of praying with her hands clasped and her eyes tightly shut. Daisy jumped and moaned whenever lightning hit and put her hands over her ears at the booming thunder that followed. The girl was so agitated by the hurricane, it was getting on Veronique's nerves...and Nick's. She could tell he was furious at not one, but two women encroaching on his privacy.

When the eye of the storm arrived, everything grew calm. Veronique dialed Natasha's number again, but to no avail. Exasperated, she got up and headed toward the door.

"Hey, where are you going?" Nick called out.

"I need to stretch for a bit. I'm going back to bed," Veronique said.

"I'd rather you stayed here until it's over."

She remained standing. "I have enough time to get to my room. I'm going to keep calling Tash until I can get through. Maybe I'll have better reception there."

"You probably will," Daisy piped in.

What did she know? Veronique could be staying in any of the five bedrooms. No doubt she'd love to get rid of her and sit beside Nick, sheltered by his broad shoulders.

Veronique wanted to strangle her.

"Stay." One word, but Nick's brisk command didn't go unnoticed. He was clearly out of patience. He turned to Daisy. "You too."

"I am not moving until you say so, Señor Nicky," Daisy simpered in a solicitous voice that didn't fool Veronique one bit. "Oops, I'm sorry. I know you don't like me to call you that. I won't do it again."

Earlier, Daisy had acted like a nervous Nellie, shuddering and wringing her hands whenever a crack of lightning slashed through the house. Now she was acting submissive and remorseful to gain points with Nick. Her playacting was enough for Veronique to grit her teeth and sit back down.

She could barely make out Nick's profile in the tension-filled, dark room, but his bridled energy was that of a stallion chomping at the bit to burst from a pen. She couldn't blame him. Being confined in the room with Daisy's jumpy nerves was stifling, not to mention irksome. The only good thing about Daisy being there was that her presence kept Nick from asking Veronique questions she wasn't ready to answer.

Something horrible has happened. Natasha's anguished words haunted Veronique. Was Tash injured? Could there be any connection with the random gunshot in the Miami parking lot?

Maybe that shot hadn't been random after all…

CHAPTER 7

By the time Hurricane Abby finished wreaking havoc on Nick's property, it left a mess behind. Veronique circled the outside of the house with Nick, checking for damage. Avocados, key limes, carambola and bunches of dwarf bananas lay heaped on the ground. Masses of wet, torn leaves, broken branches and uprooted, downed trees created hurdles as they made their way through the mud. She was glad when Nick told her that Daisy was in the kitchen making breakfast.

"You're lucky it was only a category one hurricane," Veronique said.

"Yeah. Good thing the roof is metal. It held up pretty well," Nick said, glancing at the roof.

Veronique shaded her eyes from the sun as she peered up at it.

At the front porch, they found substantial damage where an old oak tree had fallen against the wooden balustrade. Remnants of railing stuck out like spikes in the beaten down croton bushes several feet away.

Veronique cast a look at Nick's face. He'd been quiet for most of their walk.

"Did you get a hold of Natasha?" he asked, meeting her gaze.

She couldn't see his eyes behind his dark aviator shades, but from the tone of his voice, she was certain they were somber.

"Not yet. Every time I try to dial out, I get a message that all circuits are busy."

He rubbed a hand over his face. "My phone's not working either. I haven't been able to reach Fred."

"Why do you have to reach Fred?"

He gave her an incredulous look. "Why do you think? Has it occurred to you that he and your mom might be worried?"

She stiffened. He didn't know that she was estranged from both of them. Well, not exactly estranged, but she preferred to keep her distance, especially from Fred.

"I'll take care of contacting Maman. Don't call Fred on my behalf," she said emphatically. She'd never accepted Fred as her stepfather and didn't call him that. To her, he was just Fred the intruder. As a child she'd deeply resented him for selling their home and moving her mom to New York.

He had shipped Veronique off to an exclusive girl's boarding school in Virginia and had paid for her education, including a BA at Georgetown University and an MA at Northwestern in Journalism. When she found out Fred had funded her education, she vowed never to accept another penny from him. She probably should have been thankful for his assistance, but she blamed the dominant man for tearing her away from her mother's side and banishing her to boarding school. During that time, Fred took over caring for Helene full-time by marrying her.

"Why do you still resent your stepfather after all this time? He did you a big favor by sending you to boarding school."

Nick didn't understand where she was coming from. Naturally, he'd side with Fred, Helene's savior. "Not quite. Why do you say that?" she asked, not hiding her resentment.

"Your mom had a nervous breakdown. That's not a good environment for a thirteen-year-old."

"I would have been fine," Veronique stubbornly replied. Her

heart ached at the memory of being sent away so soon after Daddy's death. She had felt gutted over the loss and very out of place in the prissy all-girl boarding school. "Fred just wanted to get rid of me."

"That's not fair, Ronnie. He loves you."

She looked heavenward and waved a dismissive hand.

Nick's hands wrapped around her shoulders and squeezed lightly. "He's a good man. I respect the hell out of him. You should too." He dropped his hands to his sides as he waited for her answer.

Veronique didn't want to argue with Nick about her stepdad. Her relationship with Fred was formal and cordial at best. No matter how much Maman tried to bring them together, he'd always be the one who had separated them. They might not be similar in personality and style, but Veronique loved Maman, and she couldn't help blaming Fred for all the time she'd spent away from home in the stifling boarding school run by an oppressively strict staff. Most of the girls had spent their time obsessing about boyfriends and getting married. Not her, she'd spent her time plotting how soon she could leave and spread her wings.

A trickle of sweat slid between Veronique's breasts and also down her spine. It felt hot already, yet it was only eight o'clock in the morning. By noon, sweltering, humid heat would engulf them and unfortunately, the power hadn't been restored. She'd changed from Nick's T-shirt to the sundress she'd arrived in. Light as it was, the fabric felt sticky against her warm skin. She wished she could dive in the pool and cool off, but it was filled with the storm's debris.

If the roads into town looked anything like his yard, it would be few days before she'd be able to venture into town. That meant more time with Nick.

Nick ran a hand across the back of his neck. "Let's go inside and listen to the news. Soon as the roads are cleared and the causeway is open, you're heading back."

Gosh, it was as if he'd just read her thoughts. Veronique's heart sank at his resolute tone. Why couldn't the stubborn man chill and let her stay a little longer?

"You sound like a broken record. I already agreed to go back. You don't have to keep reminding me," she grumbled.

"Good," he grunted. "It's not that I haven't enjoyed seeing you again, Ronnie. I just need to be alone."

Her mood lightened when he admitted he'd enjoyed seeing her again. She smiled and didn't budge an inch as she stood before him. Nick didn't move a muscle either. Her gaze caught on his mouth, and she swallowed a pleasurable sigh at the thrilling memory of his kiss last night. Her glance lowered to the smooth brown column of his neck. He had felt strong and solid with her arms wrapped around him. The vivid memory made her want to wrap her arms around him now.

Nick's bronze chest and wide shoulders rocked her senses. He was brown all over, his body a beautiful array of sinew, ridges and well-defined muscle. She'd had a hard time keeping her eyes averted when he'd walked out this morning clad only in a pair of faded, low rise jeans.

She sucked in a breath and took in her fill of his male beauty. She would have loved to glide her hand over his chiseled torso. She felt his penetrating eyes on the top of her head. When she glanced up, her mouth parted and her breath came in shallow pants as she gazed at him, wide-eyed and tingling with desire.

"Don't look at me that way." Nick's voice held a compelling edge.

Her breath hitched in her chest. "Why not?" she asked softly, not taking her eyes from his mouth. She took a step closer and waited.

"We're not going there again." His voice sounded low and gravelly...and *hot*.

She knew he was referring to their kisses last night. Disappointment over his restraint made her heart sink.

She shook her head ruefully. "You have more willpower than I do. I liked last night." She touched the side of his face and hoped with all her heart he'd kiss her again. But when his mouth tightened, she removed her hand. "I wish Daisy hadn't shown up and ruined everything."

"She's going home today," he stated evenly.

"Good. Glad to hear it, Señor Nicky," Veronique said in a playful tone.

Nick pulled his sunglasses off and met her gaze with blistering blue fire. "I'm not in the mood for jokes."

Her face heated up instantly. "Sorry, I couldn't help it. I didn't mean to annoy you." The problem with Nick's no-nonsense personality was that it often tempted her to tease him. This was not a good time for that. Definitely not.

"I'm curious about Daisy. How old is she?"

"Twenty-four."

"Really? She looks younger." Veronique searched his face for a reaction, but he remained impassive. "How long has she been working for you?"

"Long enough to know she'd better quit calling me Señor Nicky if she wants to keep her job," he said in a tone so disgusted, Veronique had to swallow a giggle rising inside her. She managed to squelch it, but the corners of her mouth turned upward.

"She's sneaky about getting her way. If she wasn't such a good cook and excellent housekeeper, I'd let her go," he said.

"I'm sure you could find someone just as good," Veronique said casually.

"She needs the money to support her baby. She lives with her dad, who's my gardener. Felipe's a decent, hardworking man and he's got his hands full with her and his grandson. Daisy is too damned impulsive." He paused and slanted a meaningful look at her.

She lifted a challenging brow. "You think I'm too impulsive? Is that what you're—"

The rest of her words halted when she saw a man heading toward them with a machete. Nick's back was turned to him, but Veronique saw he was a swarthy man in combat fatigues and dirt-encrusted field boots.

CHAPTER 8

"*N*ick. Who's that with the machete?" Veronique said from of the corner of her mouth.

Nick turned around and surprised her by waving at the approaching man.

"You know him?"

"Yeah, he's the gardener." Nick strode up to the gardener and clapped him on the shoulder. "Felipe, you're just the man I wanted to see."

Felipe nodded. "I'm here to help, but first I have to find Daisy. Is she here?"

Nick frowned. "Yeah, she's here. Didn't you know?"

"No. I told her not to go to your house. She must have walked all the way over." He raised his hands in a gesture of despair. "Or hitched a ride."

"I had no idea your daughter was here until she came running out of the guesthouse last night when a tree hit the window."

Felipe's ire dissolved into fatherly concern. "Was she hurt?"

"No, she's fine. Sorry, Felipe. Daisy told me you knew she was here."

Felipe's face and neck turned red. "I didn't. Where is she?"

"In the kitchen. Come on," Nick said in a resigned tone.

Felipe set the machete down and muttered in Spanish under his breath.

Nick motioned toward Veronique. "By the way, this is Veronique Whitcomb. She's visiting from New York."

"Nice to meet you," Felipe mumbled, clearly agitated and not up to meeting anyone.

"Same here," Veronique said brightly. She was more than pleased to meet him. His arrival would take Daisy out of their hair.

THEY FOUND Daisy in the kitchen at the gas stove with Baxter at her feet. The tempting aroma of sizzling bacon, fried eggs and freshly brewed coffee made Veronique's stomach growl.

Daisy's back was turned as she slid the eggs onto a white ceramic platter. Wearing skimpy red shorts and a snug white tank top, her round hips jiggled to the beat of the Spanish song she sang in a throaty voice. An apron was tied around her waist and her long black ponytail reached the apron ties just above her behind. The edge of her shorts barely covered where her full bottom cheeks met curvy thighs, and the girl's firm, golden flesh didn't have an ounce of cellulite.

Was this Daisy's usual work attire? Veronique hoped not. Nick was sure getting an eyeful today. She stole a glance at him, fully expecting his eyes to be glued to Daisy Duke's provocative posterior, but they weren't. His attention was on Felipe, who looked spitting mad.

"Daisy! What are you doing here?" Felipe demanded.

In mid-song, Daisy whirled around and greeted her father with a sassy smile. "Oh, hi, Papi. I was making breakfast for Señor Nick."

She held up the platter of eggs and bacon. Ignoring her

father's irate face, she carried it to the kitchen table and set it down.

"Look," Daisy said, pointing to the nicely set table.

"I told you not to come here last night!" Felipe thundered in Spanish. "Why did you lie to me?"

Daisy darted a mortified glance at Nick. "I didn't lie. I was going to stay with Doña Miriam like I told you, but when I got to her house, her son had already taken her to Fort Myers."

They argued in rapid fire Spanish and Veronique understood most of it. From the annoyed look on his face, Nick did too.

Felipe's dark eyes glowered with censure. "Your mother spoils you too much, watching your baby and making life easy. You should have been home taking care of Manolito. He's sick."

Daisy quickly switched to English. "Mami knows better how to take care of him. Don't be mad, Papi. I came to help Señor Nick. He's been so generous with us—" she said, giving Nick a sidelong glance from beneath her curly lashes.

"Yes, *too* generous with you. You will work clearing the yard with me today," Felipe said firmly.

"No! You know I hate to work outside." Daisy's hands formed fists at her sides as she stood in rigid defiance before her father. The nostrils of her tip-tilted nose flared and her cheeks turned crimson beneath flashing eyes. "Señor Nick needs me here," she said, gesturing toward the pans on the stove.

"Don't worry about that. I can help with the housework," Veronique interjected, eliciting a raised brow from Nick.

Daisy gave her a hate stare. "You?" she spat out scornfully.

"Be quiet," Felipe commanded his daughter.

Baxter's ears pulled back and he began to growl.

"I'll say what I want." Daisy untied her apron, tossed it to the floor and ran toward the door. Baxter got up from his prone position and followed.

"Come back here, Bax," Nick commanded. The lab came to his

side and nudged Nick's hand with his snout. He patted the top of Baxter's head. "Good boy."

Felipe yelled after Daisy, "Where are you going?"

A slammed door was her only response as she flew outside.

Felipe turned to Nick. "I apologize for Daisy. She acts like a child sometimes. She's nineteen and should know better!" Red-faced, he retreated from the kitchen.

Nick looked disgusted when Felipe closed the door. "*Nineteen?* Hell, she lied about that too. I knew she was taking night classes at the junior college, but I had no idea she was so young."

Veronique raised her eyebrows. "Why would she tell you otherwise?" she asked as she filled two mugs with steaming coffee from the stovetop percolator and joined him at the table. If Daisy was taking night classes, she must have been a good student in high school.

Nick shrugged. "Beats me." He took the outstretched mug from her. "Aah," he said, inhaling the strong aroma. "She makes good coffee though. Let's eat."

"Hold it. We have to conserve water. Let's use the paper plates I brought." Veronique made short work of replacing the dishes with paper plates and the flatware with plastic utensils.

She slowly chewed a strip of perfectly crisp bacon while she watched Nick dig into his food with gusto. The recent exchange between Daisy and her dad had left a bad taste in her mouth. Nick, on the other hand, was relishing his breakfast.

"Gotta hand it to her. Daisy *is* a good cook, even though she doesn't tell the truth," Veronique acknowledged. She raised her brows and met his gaze. "She was cooking up more than break-fast in that outfit. Felipe looked furious."

"Can't say that I blame him. She shouldn't have lied." Nick set his fork down and splayed his hands out in a stretch. "There's too much damn drama going on around here. That girl is outta control."

No kidding. From the way Nick acted toward Daisy, she

surmised they hadn't slept together—yet. Daisy was sixteen years younger than Nick, but she was out to seduce him. Why else would she cook in such revealing shorts? The baby doll she'd worn last night had been practically see-through—good thing they'd been in the dark. This morning, Daisy had been wearing pink lip gloss and gold hoop earrings. Who wore earrings and make-up after a hurricane, for God's sake?

Veronique fed Baxter a piece of her bacon. "How did she come to be your housekeeper? Did she ask for the job?"

"She didn't have to. When I saw her working in the yard with a pregnant belly, I brought her inside to work."

Her heart fluttered as she gazed at him tenderly. She had a soft spot for Nick's innate compassion. It knocked her off her feet every time—especially now. What a dichotomy—a successful corporate raider who was capable of compassion. No wonder Zack and Elizabeth had thought they could destroy him.

"That was kind of you," she said.

"I'm not the same guy at camp, Ronnie," Nick said, his tone flat.

"You're still kind," she persisted, smiling at him.

He rolled his shoulders and stretched his neck from side to side, working out the kinks. "I wouldn't call it being kind. I needed a housekeeper and she fit the bill. I had sunk down real low, drinking too much and sleeping too much."

"When was this?" she asked, hating to imagine Nick like that.

"Six months ago. I was a mess and this place was a shambles."

"Oh, I'm sorry to hear that. What made you clean up?"

"I didn't want to end up like my old man. He was a nasty, mean drunk. The day Mom left him and took my sister and I with her is the day I started living without fear."

"I hear you," Veronique said with a heavy sigh. "My dad wasn't a mean drunk, just a sloppy one. I hated to see him stumbling around." When her famous father had drunk too much he'd became a drooling, crass man who couldn't keep his balance. She shuddered at the memory.

"Not a pretty sight for a little girl," Nick commiserated, shaking his head.

"Yes, but when Daddy was sober, he was awesome." She couldn't help feeling bad that she'd brought to light her father's tragic flaws. "Every morning, we'd have breakfast together and instead of reading the paper, he'd give me his full attention. He always asked, 'What good thing are you planning on doing today, Ronnie?' He was big on social reform. So am I."

"Really? I hadn't noticed," he said dryly.

She tapped his hand. "You're one to talk. You have a strong social conscience too."

Nick didn't respond to that, just sat there gazing at her with an unreadable expression.

She sighed. "Luckily, I only saw Daddy in bad form a few times because I had a ridiculously early bedtime."

"I never had a bedtime. What time was yours?"

"Nine o'clock. Nanny Millie was a real drill sergeant. No amount of pleading or arguing changed her mind. But when she left the room and got out of my hair, I would read till midnight," she said with a triumphant grin.

He nodded. "Just like when you were in camp."

Astonished that he'd bring it up, she said, "You remember that?"

"The only time you were quiet was when you were reading or drawing. Are you still drawing caricatures?"

She chuckled. "Absolutely. They're my wicked form of ther-apy...and revenge."

"I better not catch you drawing pictures of me," he growled, eyes darkening to midnight blue. He braced his forearms on the table with fingers laced together as he held her gaze.

"You wound me, Nick. Don't look at me that way. I'm inno-cent," she said, ignoring the twinge of guilt. If he only knew the sketch she'd been planning of him covered in plaster. He'd looked so ferocious—and cute. A big, grouchy bear dusted in snow. "Back to Daisy. I take it she got your house in order."

He pushed back in his chair and folded his arms over his chest. "You could say that. Within a week of hiring her, everything was spotless and organized. She cooked up some fine meals too. That girl loves to cook and is a clean freak. It's the only reason I've kept her on."

"I'm not exactly Suzie Homemaker, so I can't fault you there," Veronique said with a wry smile. "Frankly, I'd much rather work outside. Housework is boring."

"And yet you offered to do it just to get rid of Daisy. How generous of you." Nick's lips curved upward and the hard planes of his face softened, making her wish he'd kiss her again.

"Somebody had to get rid of her," she said, not taking her eyes from his.

"You don't pull any punches, do you, Ronnie?" The flash of appreciation in his eyes sent a ripple of pleasure through her.

"Nope. My lack of a filter has gotten me in trouble a few times," she admitted, returning his warm smile. Her heart did a little dance, relishing their moment together. They'd shared a good meal and he was opening up to her. The ever-present wariness in his eyes had lessened, making him appear more relaxed, even approachable.

"I'll bet," he grunted.

"You don't pull any punches either, Nick."

He grew silent as he regarded her across the table with brooding eyes.

Veronique lowered her gaze and collected her wits. When she looked up, he was still watching her beneath hooded lids. "So... where's the father of the baby? Is Daisy married?"

"No. He wants to marry her, but she refuses."

Veronique leaned in. "Really? Why?"

Nick shrugged and his face shuttered, signaling the subject

was closed. "Who knows? It's none of my business...or yours. Don't put your reporter hat on, Ronnie."

Holding his mug in his hand, he rose from the table and deposited it in the sink.

So much for their moment. Disappointed, Veronique drained her coffee and pushed back from the table. Baxter roused from his nap on the floor and went to his water bowl, where he slurped noisily.

"I'm going to try to reach Natasha again. Leave everything there. I'll clean up," she said, gathering the paper plates and plastic forks.

"Sure you can handle it? It might be too boring," Nick taunted.

"Oh shut up," she said, grinning.

She turned on her heel and sauntered away. After Daisy's ample display in the short shorts, she felt a bit lacking in the way of curves. But Nick was male, and she was sure he'd be looking at her retreating backside and legs.

Might as well give him something to watch. She threw in a little extra hip swaying and glanced over her shoulder.

Sure enough, he was checking her out. Her stomach did a neat flip flop as her pulse kicked up a notch.

CHAPTER 9

*N*ick shook his head and tamped down his body's instant reaction to Ronnie's saucy exit. She was going to be his undoing. He knew she was trouble from the moment she appeared at his door and he sent her away. He didn't want anyone in his house, especially not a reporter. But she'd come back like a wet, injured kitten and he'd had to let her stay. What was he supposed to do—turn her away when the bridges were closed? And besides, she was Ronnie. The girl wore her heart on her sleeve and she didn't have a mean or deceptive bone in her body.

And she believed the best in him, making it harder to turn her away.

Ronnie was too damn sexy. She reminded him of a playful little cat, clawing at him to get attention and then rewarding him with soft cuddles when she got it. He thought of the silken feel of her skin, how sweet and addictive her mouth had been when he'd kissed her…and her recent sexy strut. A shot of pure, hot desire tightened his loins and his jaw clamped down. *Don't go there.*

She had told him, "If you're fire, I want to get burned." Ronnie made no bones about wanting intimacy, but he couldn't let it happen. She might think she could handle it, but his fire would burn them both. Her inherent trust and respect touched him, made him want to open up, but he wasn't going to go down the road of seduction. Not with her.

Underneath her bravado and impulsiveness, lay a young girl's heart. He wasn't about to break it to slake his lust. He wasn't husband material and at twenty-eight, it was time for Ronnie to be thinking about marriage and having a family. Something he wasn't about to offer—no matter how enticing she was or how engaging her company.

More determined than ever to banish temptation from his mind's eye, he headed out the door toward the guesthouse.

The guesthouse was a detached structure from the main house the size of a small apartment with one bedroom, a tiny kitchen and a full bathroom. The moment he opened the door, muddy water mixed with leaves and twigs rushed out. He waded through several inches of it before he reached the window. Branches of a fallen black olive tree were stuck inside and had broken the window ledge. Slats of wood that had blown in from the force of the wind covered the rain drenched mattress.

No wonder Daisy had been scared out of her wits. Damn foolish girl. She'd narrowly escaped being killed by the tree. Felipe was right to be steamed. She had no business sneaking in last night. He'd read her the riot act later.

The grinding sound of a chainsaw caught his attention. He peered through the other bedroom window and saw Felipe hard at work, chopping a fallen tree trunk.

Nick headed outside. "Felipe!" he shouted, closing the distance between them.

Felipe looked up and shut off the chainsaw.

"How bad were the roads coming over here?" Nick asked.

Felipe wiped his sweaty brow with his shirt sleeve. "Bad. Really bad. A lot of fallen trees and garbage."

"I figured as much." Nick let out an exasperated breath. "Don't work here anymore. I'd rather you concentrate on clearing the roads today, but first I need you to remove the tree that crashed into the guesthouse."

"*Sí.* Manuel and I have been working since the sun went up to clear the road here." He gulped down water from his canteen.

"Where's Manuel?"

"In the truck, waiting for Daisy," Felipe muttered. He took his straw hat off and slapped it against his thigh, shaking off the sawdust before putting it back on his head.

"Where did you park?"

"About fifty feet up the road. Over there." He pointed to the right where a heap of pine trees had toppled across the dirt road.

DAISY BURNED with fury at her stupid father. She raced down the road blinking back blinding tears of resentment. As she rounded the bend, she slowed down when she saw Papi's old truck. She felt like slashing his tires and leaving him stranded. It would serve him right for humiliating her in front of Nick and that bitch who thought she had a claim on him! Just knowing that she was eating the fine breakfast Daisy had made for Nick made her wish she'd poisoned Veronique's portion.

It infuriated her that the bitch was a tough adversary. She and Nick must have already slept together. The thought made her stomach clench into a tight knot. Why else would she have been wearing his T-shirt and in his bedroom last night? By now she was probably rearranging his house...and his life. She had even offered to clean his house just to get rid of Daisy.

That one had to go. Daisy needed to step up her game and set her plan in motion, but first she had to send Veronique out of Nick's life and out of his home. The sooner the better before she took over and ruined everything that Daisy had set up.

Maybe poison wasn't such a bad idea. She'd read about the use of cyanide to...

Manuel stepped out of the clearing and grabbed her around the waist, knocking the wind out of her as he interrupted her thoughts.

"Slow down, *chica*. What are you running from?" he asked, pulling her closer.

Daisy shrieked and shoved at his chest with all her might. "What are you doing here? Let go of me!"

"What the hell's wrong with you?" He tightened his hold. "Why are you crying?"

"What do you care?" Daisy snarled. She swiped at her stinging eyes and struggled against his hold, but he held fast. "I said let go!"

Manuel shook her slightly. "Tell me what's wrong."

"Papi expects me to work in the yard like a field hand," she spat out.

She grimaced at the thought of sun burning her flawless complexion and she hated dirtying her nicely manicured nails. She always wore gloves to clean house. There was no way she'd ruin her hands with manual labor.

Manuel searched her face, his mouth twisting with irony. "Is that why you're crying?"

She looked away from the mocking glint in his dark eyes. He was the *last* person she wanted to see her doing yard work, getting all sweaty and grimy. She might not want to marry him, but he sure was amazing in bed.

His lean, brown fingers tweaked her gold hoop earring. "You'll survive, *princesa*. Felipe and I will do the heavy work. All you have to do is rake and help clean up."

"I'm not going to do it," she snapped.

Manuel's generous lips curved upward to reveal white teeth vividly contrasting against dark olive skin. His eyes flashed with amusement as his rough-skinned hands lowered to her hips and anchored her before him.

"Doesn't suit your fancy style, huh, Princess Daisy?"

Daisy thrust her chin up and her mouth turned downward with scorn. "That's right and don't forget it. One day I'm going to have a big house like Nick's, and I won't answer to Papi...or a laborer like you." She gestured to his work clothes with a derisive twist of her lips.

His smile faded and his black eyes hardened. "You're wrong, *chica*. We have a son."

She tossed her head. "So? We're not married. I'm free."

"When I finish my night classes, I'll get a real job and we'll get married," he stated arrogantly.

"Don't count on it." She was taking night classes too. It would be a long road before she got the power and wealth she craved... unless she seduced Nick and got him to marry her.

Manuel's mouth twisted. "Shut up. You're rude and spoiled. I don't want you raising our son to be that way."

His eyes raked over her. He was too hard to ignore—his eyes too scorching, his mouth too sexy, his lean muscles too tempting...too bad he would never be as rich or as powerful as Nick. She hated that her body was already heating up at the feel of Manuel's strong hands on her hips. A surge of eagerness made her squeeze her thighs together to stop them from quivering. *Damn him, she was already wet.*

"As long as I'm alive, we are connected." Manuel pressed her against his swollen erection. "I'll see you tonight."

His rough hands cupped her buttocks, gave them a hard squeeze and released her. Daisy fought the hot tremor of lust coursing through her. Tight-lipped, she watched him stalk toward the house.

Bastard.

CHAPTER 10

*A*fter she washed the pans, Veronique tried calling Natasha again, but to no avail. She would try all day until she finally got through. Setting her phone down, she got her toiletries together and headed toward the master bathroom. She stripped and stepped into the stall, gasping when the cold water hit her hot skin. She sucked in shaky breaths as her body adjusted to the shock of frigid water. Turning her face toward the shower-head, her chest heaved with shallow puffs as she tried to catch her breath. She quickly soaped up and rinsed off using the hand held shower nozzle. She shaved her legs too, just in case…

Satisfied she was clean and presentable, she cut the shower short to conserve water. They hadn't gotten word of water contamination yet, but it could happen at any time. At least there was enough water pressure for a decent shower.

Back in the guest bedroom, she rubbed her favorite honey almond scented body cream all over, luxuriating in its lush fragrance. It was her portable aromatherapy—lightweight, yet rich enough to leave her skin moisturized and satiny. It always made her feel good.

Pulling her hair up in a high ponytail, she dressed in a cool summer dress and flat sandals, opting for the barest clothes to deal with the heat streaming into the house. The power was out and the radio announcer had said it might take weeks to be restored.

Nick had taken the shutters down early in the morning. She opened all the windows in her room to air it out, welcoming the bright sunlight as it streamed in. The sun never failed to lift her spirits.

Through the bedroom window she saw Nick working on the lawn and wondered where Felipe and Daisy had gone. Sunlight glinted on his chiseled physique, making him look like sculpted marble. His skin was tanned an even rich brown and tautly stretched over the muscle and sinew of his back and powerful arms. He was too gorgeous not to record. On impulse, she pulled her camera out of her purse and zoomed in. She filmed him at every angle, including close-ups of his face in deep concentration as she narrated, "Hurricane Abby tore apart Nick's paradise, but that hasn't deterred him. He's powerful and unstoppable." The minute she said that, she felt a stab of guilt. She had told him she wouldn't take more pictures. This wasn't exactly breaking her promise though—nobody would see it. The homage to Nick's male beauty was for her eyes only.

When she was satisfied she'd gotten some priceless footage to treasure later, she turned away from the window and took her notebook out. In times of stress, her work was her refuge. She immersed herself in writing a detailed report on Hurricane Abby. When she finished, she gave into the impulse to draw a caricature of Nick just as he'd looked in the closet covered in white dust. By the time she completed the drawing, she was in stitches.

Nick didn't come in until late afternoon. His blue eyes glittered vibrantly against his tan and the sexy stubble on his jaw. She was in the kitchen getting ready to heat up dinner when he strolled by holding two buckets.

"What've you got there?" she asked.

"Bananas, avocados and key limes," he said, lifting one bucket. He lifted the other bucket, drawing her attention to his flexed biceps. "This one has fish I caught for our dinner."

Yikes! She had never cooked fish in her life. She wasn't about to experiment now. "Um...I hate to tell you this, but I've never cleaned a fish before, let alone cooked one."

"You can always learn." His eyes glinted with challenge.

"I guess..." she said hesitantly. *Yuck*, the last thing she wanted to do was cut a fish's head off and...

He gave a short bark of laughter.

"What's so funny?"

"You should see your face," he said, his mouth twitching with amusement. "Don't worry. I was planning on grilling it."

She drew in a deep sigh of relief. "You were? Will you filet it too?"

"Yeah. But first I'm going to take a shower."

"Get ready to freeze your butt off," she said with a grin. "I almost couldn't breathe this morning when the cold water hit my body."

He gave a wry twist of his mouth. "I'll survive."

She smiled. "I'll make a salad while you're showering. What else should I do? Bring you a blanket? You might need one after the cold shower."

"I doubt that. No need for a blanket tonight." He was right; the blue flame in his eyes warmed them both.

Nick smelled so good when he returned from his shower, she wanted to wrap herself around him and never let go. She loved his company. He was strong and manly, and just being with him made her heart race. It was hard to mask her pleasure.

She sat across from him at the kitchen table and squeezed key lime juice on the fish he'd grilled to perfection. She tasted her first bite and gave an appreciative moan.

"Mmm, delicious. Who knew you were a good cook?" she mused, smiling. The grilled fish, avocado and onion salad, and the rice she'd heated up on the stove made for a light, but satisfying meal.

He made a wry face. "I wouldn't exactly call myself a good cook, but I can grill anything you like, even toast."

"You can grill my toast any day, and butter it too," she said with a sassy grin.

His mouth lifted into an unexpected smile that delighted her. But it didn't last long. His face sobered as he asked, "Were you able to reach Natasha?"

"Not yet. I tried all day. It's driving me crazy that I don't know what happened. She must be beside herself trying to reach me," Veronique said, sobering from her lighthearted mood. Her stomach constricted as she remembered Natasha had said something terrible had happened.

"Yeah," he grunted. "My phone doesn't work either."

"I heard on the news that they're concentrating on getting Fort Myers back in business with power and phone service before they come to Starfish Island."

He looked unfazed. "I figured as much. We were told to evacuate."

"We'll have to make the best of it. I just hope my boss isn't mad at me."

Nick's eyes narrowed. "Why would he be mad?"

"He told me to stay in Fort Myers and report from there," she admitted. "I didn't tell him I was going to the island."

Nick shook his head. "Big surprise. You didn't listen to your boss and you ventured here instead," he said in a blunt tone.

"I'm glad I did." She jutted her chin out. "It's much more interesting on the island. I'll get better stories here," she added when he remained silent. "Are you still annoyed I'm here?"

He didn't answer, just watched her steadily. She wished she could retract the question, but it glared in the open, exposed and needy as the minutes ticked by.

"Never mind. Don't answer that," she mumbled and ate a large forkful of salad.

The firm set of his mouth relaxed. "I'm not annoyed," he finally said. "Much as I'd rather not admit it, you're good company."

That floored her. "Thank you, Nick!" She gave his cheek a resounding kiss and settled back in her chair with a wide smile. "You're good company too. The best host—and grill master ever."

He looked to the ceiling with feigned patience and ate the rest of his meal quietly. She didn't mind his silence. Her heart did silent leaps of joy. He had just admitted he enjoyed her company. Energy surged inside of her and it was all she could do to keep from bouncing around the room. If she allowed herself to jump as high as she felt, he'd have to peel her from the ceiling.

AFTER DINNER, dusk began to settle around them. Soon the house would be cloaked in darkness. Veronique cleaned the kitchen quickly and disposed of the fish remnants in a tight plastic bag so there wouldn't be any fishy smell while Nick got the lanterns ready to illuminate the inside of the house.

She was wiping the counters when he appeared in the kitchen. "Finished?" he asked.

"Yep. I'm craving a shower. I just wish it could be a warm one."

He quirked an eyebrow. "What happened to the tough reporter in Afghanistan?"

"She's sticky and hot. Frankly after seeing you bare-chested all afternoon, I need a cold shower," she quipped. She looked up at him and when she caught the half-smile on his face, her bones felt fluid. Nick's slow grin robbed any strength in her limbs.

He followed her to the master bathroom and left a lit lantern for her. "I'll be in my bedroom," he said. "Come join me after your shower."

Yes, darling, I'll be there ASAP, she thought with a giddy smile. She could barely get through the shower, she was so eager to join him in the bedroom…his bedroom. She soaped up and tried to center herself. She was dying to know what would happen next, and she didn't linger longer than necessary. After toweling off, she smoothed honey almond scented cream all over and then nabbed a white terrycloth robe from the door hook and put it on over her tank top and bikini panties.

She found Nick lying on his back in bed when she entered the master suite.

"Are you awake?" She lifted the lantern to search his face.

"Yes. Shut off the lantern and come here," he said in a low voice.

Gulp. She was rendered speechless by his command. He sure was direct. Her breath came out in a whoosh as she forced herself to walk on wobbly legs to his bed. She perched on the side, every muscle in her body tense with anticipation as she waited.

When he spoke, it wasn't what she had expected to hear, not by a long shot. "We only have one fan. The one you brought from Miami," he said, motioning to the oscillating battery-run fan facing the bed.

"Is that why you asked me to come here?"

"Yeah. The only solution is for you to sleep here. With me."

"Or?" Her stomach fluttered wildly at the thought of sleeping with him in his bed.

"There is no 'or'. It's hot and we both could use some cooling down. That's all," he said in an even tone.

Her hopes deflated like a flat tire at the matter-of-fact way he said it. "Ooookay." She tossed off her robe and got in bed before he changed his mind.

After an awkward moment, she said, "I gotta warn you, Nick. I'm a wild woman in my sleep."

"What?" he asked, his voice incredulous.

"I might hit you and not know it."

The bed shook with the rumble of his laughter.

"It's not funny. I mean it. When I wake up, my legs are usually tangled in the sheets and many times my pillows are on the floor."

"What brings that on?"

"I dream a lot, and my dreams usually involve adventures. Stuff like diving off a cliff or flying with my arms spread wide."

"Like a bird," he said in a voice choking with amusement.

"No, like superwoman," she said, deadpan. "I might sweep right over and land on top of you."

"I'll take my chances." He chuckled, the sound robustly male and enticing. "Better stay on your side for good measure."

She hit him with her pillow and then scooted back to her side of the bed. "How's this? Far enough?"

"Yeah. Go to sleep," he said gruffly.

As if that were possible with him beside her, bare-chested and smelling so good. For a long time afterward, neither spoke as they lay side by side, a foot apart. No cover sheet. She usually slept on her stomach, but not tonight. There was no way she'd turn away when all she wanted was to be as close to him as possible.

The gentle whirr of the fan mingled with the sounds of crickets and frogs outside, but she was only aware of her heart thrumming inside her chest. Lying on her back with her neck and head propped on her folded arms, she stared at the ceiling until she heard Nick's rhythmic breathing, signaling he'd fallen asleep. She rolled onto her side and watched him as the silvery moonlight illuminated his strong profile.

The hard contours of his face were relaxed now, revealing how handsome he was. His dark brows rested above lush, long lashes that hid his brilliant blue eyes and cast shadows on his sharp cheekbones. His firm mouth had softened sensuously making her wild with yearning to kiss him. Desire pulsated through her veins, profuse, sweet and urgent. She wanted Nick to be wild for her too, not only physically, but emotionally. *God, how she wished it!*

She stayed awake for a long while, wondering how long he would allow her to stay. When she couldn't stand the separation any longer, she closed the gap between them and rested her hand on his chest over his heart. She resisted the temptation to smooth her hand across the hard ridges of muscle on his broad chest. Nick's sturdy heartbeat beneath her palm pleased her beyond measure. It linked them together in a special way.

Veronique softly brushed a strand of his hair from his forehead, wishing she could run her fingers through his thick, rumpled hair. What would it take to release the tight rein Nick held on his feelings? When he didn't stir, she moved in closer. He was a deep sleeper. If he woke up during the night, he'd think she had gotten there in her sleep. Turning her face into his warm neck, she inhaled deeply and kissed the hollow at his throat. The feather light brush of her lips on his warm skin made her moan with pleasure. It robbed her of her breath and the desire to sleep. A smile lifted the corners of her mouth at the sensual heat emanating from Nick, even as he slept. Much later, she fell asleep, curled beside him and thrilled to be there.

She woke up at the feel of a large hand resting on her stomach. She froze and her eyes shot open. How long had Nick been holding her this way? Carnal energy radiated from his body behind her as she lay on her side, facing away from him. He wasn't exactly spooning her. The only part touching her was his hand. His long fingers were tucked inside the waistband of her panties, his blunt fingertips grazing her mound. Her heart reeled as acute spasms of desire rocked her.

She held her breath and didn't move a muscle as she listened to his steady breathing. He was still asleep. His warm breath fanned the back of her ear; he was that close to her. She felt him stir and slowly move his hand in a sensuous circle. Alternately squeezing and stroking, his fingers slid southward until he abruptly stopped and groaned.

Oh God, he's awake. She heard another deep, rough growl of discomfort as he lay there for what felt like a long time. Pretending to be asleep, she rolled onto her stomach and waited until he got up. With a smile, she listened to him stomp out of the room. It pleased her that he was physically affected by her. Having to lie still beside him had been like being on a sexually charged landmine.

BY THE TIME Nick came out of the bathroom, showered and dressed, Veronique was gone, but she'd left a surprise on his pillow—an irreverent caricature of him as a big, grumpy bear covered in white powder, just how he'd looked in the closet. The caption underneath said, "Patience, my ass! I'm gonna kill someone."

He threw his head back and laughed—deep, cleansing laughter that revitalized him. He put the caricature in the night-stand for safekeeping and headed outside to work, still smiling and shaking his head at her nerve.

CHAPTER 11

$\mathscr{V}$eronique phoned Natasha again, but wasn't able to connect. She was at her wits' end trying not to panic because she didn't have phone service and going nuts worrying over what Tash needed to tell her.

To distract herself, she spent most of the morning alternating between writing and doing housework. Strangely enough, she didn't mind the housework. It took the edge off her nervous energy. She even scrubbed the shower stall in the master bathroom. When she finished her chores, she drank two bottles of water, feeling like she'd finished a marathon.

Thank God, Daisy had left enough meals to last for several days. With the extra freezer in the garage filled with ice, they'd been able to salvage most of the prepared meals before Veronique would have to resort to cooking. After eating Daisy's excellent cooking, Nick wouldn't be thrilled with hers. Oh well, he'd have to make do unless he wanted to grill their food, which was fine with her.

Her parents had employed a full staff of servants and cooks. Maman had never cooked a meal in her life, and Veronique never got the opportunity to learn, until she got to college. The only things she knew how to make were easy to put together. Spaghetti with store bought marinara sauce, grilled cheese sandwiches, yogurt and fruit were her go-to meals whenever there wasn't a takeout place or pizza delivery available.

In some ways being on the island with Nick was like being on vacation and camping out, but in a mansion by the sea instead of a tent. It reminded her of her carefree jaunts as a kid, away from the confines of her parents' stuffy palatial home. She wished she could disconnect and relax completely, but she wouldn't until she was able to complete her investigation of the Cameron Hope Foundation and deliver the information to Nick—before it was too late.

By late afternoon, she was craving fresh air and ventured outside in search of Nick.

"Hi," she said when she found him working outside the guesthouse. "What can I do to help?"

"Hand me what I need while I board up this window." Poker-faced, he didn't mention the caricature, but she'd heard his hearty laughter earlier—the sweetest sound in the world. "They're in the toolbox there," he said, indicating the open metal box at his feet.

"Yes, sir. I'm happy to assist you," she drawled playfully.

He lifted a brow. "You can start by handing me the concrete nails as I ask for them."

Veronique took several nails from the open rectangular metal box on the floor and held them in her palm, handing them over one by one as he requested. It was hot and humid as she worked beside Nick, but she didn't mind. She loved spending time with him. The fact that he had allowed her to stay on, let alone sleep in his bed last night, was promising. He hadn't mentioned her leaving yet, but it had to be on his mind. Of course, leaving would have been impossible because the roads leading to the causeway were obstructed by fallen pine trees and the storm's debris.

"What's next for you when you leave here?" Nick asked.

Her eyes shot open. Was he a mind reader? It was the second

time he'd addressed something on her mind. "I'm going back to Fort Myers to interview some of the preppers. Remember the cult like group I told you about that's obsessed with emergency preparation?"

He nodded.

"I want to report on how they made out after the hurricane. There's also a group of senior citizens in Bonita Springs I want to do a story on."

"About what?" he asked between hammering nails into the wood planks covering the broken window.

"They are a growing group of baby boomers over sixty who are major party animals. They go dancing every weekend looking for fun and romance. They act much younger than their years." She tilted her head and studied him with a crinkled brow. "Do you like to dance? Come to think of it, you never danced at our camp parties."

"That's right. You couldn't get me on a dance floor."

"Aw, too bad. Not even slow dancing?" Nothing would please her more than to slow dance with Nick, pressed against his hard body as his strong arms held her close. She closed her eyes and enjoyed the tantalizing image.

"I'll slow dance, but I don't get into the other moves."

Nick's tone was so dry, Veronique chuckled. "Well, I love to dance. When I get old, I want to be like those oldie goldies who party hard. I'll be dancing and having a good time and not thinking about arthritis or the other stuff they have to deal with."

"I can just see you, white-haired and shaking your booty on the dance floor," Nick said, his mouth twitching and his eyes alight with amusement.

"Exactly. I'll take that as a compliment."

"It is," he said, rewarding her with a rare smile.

"Thanks." She smiled back, delighted by his unexpected compliment.

They segued into chatting about their college years and it

became obvious how very different his had been from hers. He'd been focused on finishing his degree and making money right away while she'd been more intent on experiencing life and relishing her newfound freedom through traveling. His drive during his college years exceeded that of most frat boys, who partied more than they studied. He'd worked on campus and completed four years of undergrad in three on a scholarship. After that, he'd gotten his MBA. He hadn't mentioned he'd graduated summa cum laude, but she knew it from Fred, his proud mentor.

Nick didn't mention Elizabeth and she didn't ask. It was a sore subject and too raw for him to discuss with her.

When he finished hammering the last nail, Nick said, "I'm done here. I'm going to pick up the fruit that fell after the storm."

"I'll help you," Veronique said. "I love fruit. What's your favorite?"

"Peaches."

"Mine too! Although whenever I pass by a peach tree I get all prickly."

"Allergies?"

"No, sore childhood memories," she said with a short laugh.

Nick's brow furrowed. "What do you mean?"

"When I was eight, Maman made me wear a prissy pink dress with ruffles so she could show me off to her book club friends. Small wonder I hate pink," she muttered. "She was hosting a high tea and everything was perfect, right down to the white-gloved maids. Course I didn't want anything to do with her tea party and her snooty friends, so I sneaked out and sat under my favorite peach tree reading a racy detective novel I'd stolen from Daddy's bookshelf and gorging on peaches."

Nick chuckled. "With your nose buried in the book."

"Exactly. I'd already devoured three peaches, when I felt a large hand on the nape of my neck. My book went flying as Nanny Jenna hauled me up in front of her. She gave me a stern lecture on not ruining my dress with sticky peach juice and grass stains, and then she switched me with a peach tree switch. I still get a prickly feeling when I see a peach tree," she said, twisting her mouth in a wry grimace.

"Ah, so that explains it," Nick said, lips twitching.

"She didn't get away with it either. I bit her leg so hard, she released me and I ran home yelling bloody murder. When I got home, Maman's guests had already left, *thank God.* She was so horrified when I showed her the stripes on my poor bottom and thighs, she fired Nanny Jenna on the spot."

"Good. That woman had no business switching you that way. It didn't work anyway, did it?" he said with a lift of his brow.

"Nope," she said, chuckling unrepentantly. "I went through a few more nannies after her."

"I'll bet. I can't blame you for gorging on the peaches though. One time my mom brought home a bushel of fresh-picked peaches a farmer had given her. I've never eaten so many in one sitting." Nick's eyes took on a bemused look, and he shook his head as if to clear the memory. His open expression closed up and he said, "I'll gather the avocados in the back yard while you work out front. Okay?"

"Sure," she agreed, guessing he was done talking. He had spent the last six months alone. She didn't want to crowd him with too much conversation.

They worked for another hour, he in the backyard and she in the front. Veronique was busy picking up key limes from the ground when two big hands grabbed her by the waist and lifted her up from behind. The fruit went flying as she was upended and suspended from the ground with her feet dangling.

Nick hefted her over his shoulder and wrapped a thick arm around her thighs, holding her in place as he strode toward the back of the house.

"Hey. What are you doing?" she squealed, wriggling on his shoulder.

"You've been working too hard in the hot sun. Time to cool off."

"Yay, where are we going?" she asked, lifting her head to see through the curtain of her disheveled hair.

"I seem to recall you love to swim," he said, heading toward the pool.

She grinned. "Why yes, I do. Are you going to join me?" she asked, bobbing on his shoulder.

"Nope." He dropped her in the pool and dusted his hands while she flailed around in the water. "Not this time, Picasso," he said, laughing as he sauntered away.

"Ahh, I take it you saw the resemblance," she called out, giggling madly.

THAT EVENING they ate reheated *arroz con pollo*, one of the many meals left by Daisy. Save for some small talk, Nick didn't say much. After dinner he told her she could have the bed to herself. He slept outside in a lounge chair beside the pool, claiming it was cooler there, and he was probably right. The air between them last night had been electrically charged and too hot to handle. Sleeping in bed with him again, without touching, seemed impossible now.

The following morning, after spending the night alone tossing and turning, she was antsy to get out and explore. Felipe had been by earlier to tell them that most of the roads leading to the bridge were cleared. Luckily, he'd come alone, without Daisy.

While Nick worked to restore the damage in the guest quarters, she made two cheddar cheese and mustard sandwiches—one for herself and one for him. She put her sandwich in a backpack along with her wallet and cell phone, a rolled up beach towel, a bottle of water, and a tube of sunscreen. She would go into town and find neighbors who'd stayed on and faced Hurricane Abby. On the way back, she promised herself a nice long swim in the ocean.

Wearing a straw hat, a pair of cut-off denim shorts, a halter top over her bikini, and toting the backpack, she headed to the guest quarters to tell Nick she was going into town. But she changed her mind in mid-stride. He might suggest it was time for her to leave for good. The thought of it made her heart hurt. She didn't want to think of leaving yet.

She turned in the opposite direction and ran to the garage where she found a road bike she could use. Feeling carefree and happy to be outdoors, she pedaled on the long dirt road leading to Begonia Way. Once there she turned left and headed into town, paying close attention to maneuvering around fallen branches and debris.

When she'd first arrived on Starfish Island, she'd noticed a small bar called Shipwreck Fuel on Begonia Way in the downtown area. It was a standalone building, brightly painted in hot pink and lime green with drawings of ships, loot and comical looking pirates on the sides. The windows had been boarded up in preparation of the storm. If she was lucky, it would still be there and the locals would be gathered around swapping hurricane stories.

No such luck. When she got there, the front door was off the hinges, the Shipwreck Fuel sign on the floor, and the inside walls and floor looked like they'd sustained major flooding. But true to human nature, a group of five people sat on barstools under two huge beach umbrellas where a makeshift bar was set up. The bar consisted of a plank of wood hoisted on two columns of concrete blocks and covered with an assortment of liquor bottles and plastic cups. Beside the bar was a large cooler on wheels that looked promising.

She rummaged in her backpack for her camera and wanted to smack herself when she realized she left it at home. She was thankful Nick hadn't confiscated it again after that night in the closet. He'd been too preoccupied with the hurricane since. She could only hope he wouldn't remember.

Manning the bar was a deeply tanned, middle-aged woman in a bright floral muumuu. Her white blonde hair was pulled up in a tight topknot on the crown of her head with the fried ends sticking out.

"Welcome. You look like you could use a drink," she boomed in a deep-throated voice suited to coaching sports. She eyed Veronique up and down with a friendly smile.

"Any chance I can get a cold drink?" Veronique said.

"Sure thing. I've got a generator at home. This cooler is full of ice and cold beer," the woman said, flashing a white, gap-toothed grin. "What'll you have?"

"I'd die for a cold beer."

"You got it. That'll be five dollars," the woman said briskly as she handed her a chilled longneck.

Veronique pulled six dollars out of her pocket and set it on the counter. With a happy sigh, she took a long, satisfying swig of cold beer straight from the bottle. The icy bubbles refreshed her parched throat and before she knew it, she'd chugged it all down. The alcohol hit her empty stomach with a bang and she suddenly felt lightheaded. She should have eaten something more substantial than a cranberry nut granola bar before leaving. Now she craved a burger or even a hot dog to go along with the beer instead of the cheese sandwich in her bag. Given the noontime heat, it was probably a grilled cheese sandwich by now.

"What's your name?" the woman asked Veronique as she handed her a paper napkin.

Veronique blotted her lips with the napkin. The woman was so friendly and direct, she couldn't help liking her. "Veronique Whitcomb. What's yours?"

"Sadie Green, owner of the heap behind you," she said, jerking her thumb toward the now defunct bar.

"Glad to meet you, Sadie."

Sadie nodded. "Likewise. This is Ron and that's Linda," she said, motioning toward a young couple across from Veronique. The couple nodded a greeting, but kept to themselves. She gestured to the remaining three at the bar. "That's Rafael and Juanita. They work for Ron and Linda," she said, pointing her chin toward a couple drinking what looked like *Cuba libres*, rum and cola.

"Hi," Veronique said. They acknowledged her greeting with a smile and a raised hand.

"And that's my husband, Jerry," Sadie said, waving a freckled hand at the pot-bellied man who looked like a sea captain with his shock of white hair, leathery skin and white beard.

"Nice to meet all of you," Veronique said, noting the curious looks they gave her.

"Where are you staying?" Jerry asked, leaning back to study her as he puffed on a stinky cigar.

"I came from Fort Myers. I was dropped off by a colleague who has a boat there."

"And you brought a bike with you?" Sadie asked with a puzzled look.

"Yes, I figured it would be a good way to get around."

Sadie nodded. "I could use a bike right about now. Fuel is precious and I don't want to use it up. We need it for our boats and to run the generator."

Veronique smiled. "I'm a reporter for Ace News. I'd love to talk to you about why you stayed behind even under mandatory evacuation orders."

"Jer and I have lived here for the past fifty years. The last hurricane that came by was Hurricane Charley. It was a cat four and we weathered it just fine," Sadie said emphatically.

"What about this time?" Veronique asked, pulling a notebook and pen out of her backpack. "How did you make out after the hurricane?"

"We survived just like we did the last one." Sadie shook her head and clicked her teeth. "Lotsa hoopla for nothing. Why just this morning I was telling Jer that…"

Veronique let the woman talk as she scribbled notes for a story.

ALL MORNING, Nick worked on pulling up the wooden planks that had buckled from the flooding. When hunger pangs reminded him it was lunchtime, he went to the kitchen in search of Veronique. One large, wrapped sandwich on a paper plate sat on the table beside a thermos of coffee and a mug. She'd left a scribbled note on the sandwich anchored down with a toothpick. The note said, "Going to explore. I'll be back in time for dinner," nothing else.

He went straight to the guest room where she kept her things. The moment he entered it, her almond scent filled his nostrils. She had a maddening habit of slathering her skin with a scented body cream that knocked his socks off…and perfumed his sheets at night. Having her in his bed, all soft curves, creamy skin and smelling like honeyed almonds was like having a succulent dessert handed to you with a warning to look, but not taste. Ronnie was too soft and appealing to ignore and her body was slim, curvy and toned all over—just how he liked a woman's body to be.

He could still feel her silky skin when he'd laid his hand on the slight curve of her belly. When she'd turned on her stomach, hugging her pillow with one slender leg bent at the knee, her sheer bikini panties had hiked up to reveal the sweet curve of her pert bottom. He'd broken out in a cold sweat as his body reacted swiftly and powerfully. It had taken every ounce of grit and willpower to get out of bed and ignore the throbbing ache that made him want to take her right here. Setting his jaw, he forced her delectable image from his mind.

She must have left right after breakfast. She hadn't taken the rental car; it was where he'd left it before the hurricane. Her suit-case was still in the bedroom so she obviously meant to return. She wasn't the neatest person, but he didn't care. Her flip flops were haphazardly strewn on the floor—one beside the bed and the other next to the desk. Her tank top and panties were flung on the chair in front of the desk that faced the window. She must have changed in a hurry and left.

He headed outside and checked the double car garage. He found his Land Rover and Vespa there, but noticed his road bike was missing. He usually parked it beside the Vespa and the space was empty now.

A sharp twinge of disappointment made him realize he missed her. It annoyed him that she'd left like that without letting him know first. He was getting used to having her around. Well, not exactly used to it, more like looking forward to it. She had gotten to him all right. Her saucy smile and twinkling emerald eyes lightened his mood. Not once in the past year had he laughed like he had when he'd seen the caricature she left on his pillow. His laughter had awakened a part of him that had lain dormant for too long—the fun of kicking back and enjoying the lighter side of life.

Spontaneous, spirited and unpredictable, Veronique was like a colorful rainbow after a storm. He hated having to send her back. His desire to make love to her was primal and urgent, yet when she gazed at him with those fiercely trusting eyes, he couldn't risk breaking her heart. She was becoming too attached. If they had sex, she'd never leave. He wouldn't want her to go either. But she had to. She would vehemently object and find a million reasons to stay.

It was time to send her away, off the island and back to the mainland, he decided resolutely—even if he had to take her there himself.

But first he had to find her.

CHAPTER 12

*V*eronique didn't realize how far she'd drifted into the ocean until the sound of cawing seagulls drew her attention to the sky. She'd intended to take a short swim and then a long walk along the coast to see what treasures the hurricane had washed ashore. But she ended up swimming much longer. She couldn't seem to get enough of the turquoise sea. She'd been alternating between floating and swimming, reveling in the freedom of all that expanse of water.

She had left Nick's bike under a tree next to a secluded, winding path that led to the beach. She needed to gather up her towel and backpack quickly and head back. If she got caught in a downpour, she wouldn't really mind. It might be fun to race in the rain, riding Nick's road bike the way it was meant to be ridden. It was sturdy and equipped to handle rough terrain. For the most part the roads had been cleared, save for some pieces of driftwood, stray shrubs and twigs, and rocks that she'd have to avoid.

Her frame was a tad small for his bike and reaching the pedals was a stretch, but she'd found a way to lean forward enough to handle the challenge. She'd pay for it tomorrow with sore legs and glutes, but the workout was worth it for the rush she got cruising on his bike.

Purple clouds suddenly appeared, darkening the sky. Where had they come from? When she'd started swimming, she'd felt the hot sun on her back. Now that the sun was partially covered, everything felt cooler. As the clouds gathered closer and completely covered the sun, her arms and legs paddled vigorously to reach the shore.

She swam closer to the shoreline and when it was shallow enough, she tried to get up, but her limbs gave way as the surf pulled her down. She had underestimated the stamina needed to swim in turbulent waters caused by an abrupt weather change. Between the ride into town and her long swim, she'd spent the whole day exercising and it felt good, but her muscles were fatigued. She'd pushed her body to the limit.

NICK DROVE the Land Rover down Begonia Way in search of Ronnie. When he'd left the house, the sun had been shining, but now rain clouds covered it, lowering the temperature and ushering in gusts of wind. With mounting frustration, his eyes scanned both sides of the two-lane road, hoping to catch a glimpse of her. He was about to turn in another direction, when he saw a flash of silver in a parking lot at a distance on the gulf side, near the beach.

Approaching the parking lot, he saw the silver object was his road bike resting under a bedraggled banyan tree stripped bare of leaves by the hurricane. A disturbing feeling of imminent danger snaked up his spine when he didn't see Ronnie nearby. He swerved into the lot, parked the Land Rover and bolted out.

Calling Ronnie's name, he ran down the twisting path to the beach. His mind raced with all kinds of horror when she didn't answer his calls. Was she injured? Unconscious? There were sharp rocks and snakes and the mighty ocean to contend with.

She was healthy and athletic, but it had been stupid of her to venture to the beach alone during an oncoming storm.

"Ronnie!" he roared, growing more agitated by the second. Across the expanse of white sand, he saw a figure emerge from the water. His legs propelled him forward with energy wrought from despair. The impact of his feet pounding the seashells and crushing them was nothing compared to the powerful hammering of his heart. It felt like an elephant's foot was trampling on his chest as he raced forward.

As he got closer, he saw the distinct curves of a woman's figure before she stumbled back into the water. His blood ran cold when he realized it was Ronnie. When she tried to get up again, a wave knocked her down and pulled her further back in the ocean. Her arms flailed and he heard her shout something, but her words were garbled as she sputtered with water. What the hell was she doing swimming alone when a storm was coming? There could be a riptide! Frantic to save her, he leaped across the sand like an Olympian athlete.

Nick dove in the water, swam to her and looped an arm around her neck. Propelled by a rush of adrenaline like none he'd ever felt, he swam hard and fast, pushing against the rising tide as he brought them ashore. His heart hurtling, he rose and hauled her up beside him. She slumped against him and gulped in air as she coughed. Harnessing his temper, he thumped her back between her shoulder blades to help clear her lungs.

"Whew, that was a close one," she said in a shaky voice as she straightened. "Good thing you showed up, I might not have made it."

Ronnie's bikini top had come loose, he noticed, when his gaze lowered to make sure she was all right. The neck straps of her bikini top were dangling and the small scrap of coral fabric hung around her waist. Pale and round with tight pink nipples, her pretty breasts made him go instantly hard.

She followed his fevered gaze and blushed bright red.

"Whoops. My top got loose with all that thrashing around." She turned her back to him as her shaking hands struggled to fix the straps. "Can you give me a hand here?"

"Forget it, it's broken." He spun her around by the shoulders and stared at her, furious that she could have drowned and desperate over the impact of that kind of loss. "Damn you! Don't you know better than to swim in this kind of weather?" He shook her when she didn't answer.

Her chin shot up belligerently. "Hey, don't yell! I'm not stupid. It was sunny when I got in."

There was just so much he could take. His hand wound in her wet hair as he tilted her head back and bent his head, his mouth covering hers, hard and possessive. His hands slid down and cupped her buttocks, lifting her up and anchoring her against him. Perched on her tiptoes, her thighs were nestled intimately between his.

"Nick—" she uttered in a strangled voice.

"Don't. Ever. Do that. Again," he gritted furiously between crushing kisses.

She pulled back and stared at him, her eyes huge with wonder. "So you do care, Nick Cameron."

Her words were his undoing. He swore under his breath, beyond control now. Unrestrained, primitive desire reared up inside him, making him go wild. Oblivious to the surging gulf behind them or the soft rain on his back, his mouth covered hers with an urgency born of desperation.

He could have lost her.

He'd have her now or he'd die wanting her.

NICK'S SAVAGE reaction stunned Veronique. His blue eyes gleamed in a stone hard face as he kissed her again and again. Greedy, grinding kisses that made her knees buckle and her heart beat a wild staccato. He held her steady as she opened her lips and drank in his ravenous kisses, tasting his carnal hunger, feeling his heat. The dominant intent to mate radiated in waves from his rigid body. His large hands felt like iron on her bottom as he anchored her against his solid, jutting arousal. He kissed her long and hard, sucking the very marrow from her, making her tremble with excitement when he lowered her to the sand.

He tore off his clothes while she tried to get out of her bikini. She pulled the bottoms off, but the back knot wouldn't give on the top. He yanked the ends apart and threw the top aside before taking her in his arms. Her sensitive nipples brushed against his chest and pebbled. She shivered as raw, urgent desire coursed through her veins, singeing a dangerous path to her heart. She wanted him with her whole being, was blind to everything but Nick—his male scent of arousal, the feel of his large body on hers. She had never ached so much for a man, had never yearned to give herself so fully.

The rasp of his faint beard on her soft breast made her arch to receive more as his mouth closed over her nipple and sucked deeply. The aching tip puckered in his mouth, igniting a fire deep in her belly as intense, unbearable excitement began to build. Her thighs quivered uncontrollably when his hand eased them apart and his long fingers delved into her feminine folds, caressing, stroking, until she was mindless with wanting him. His touch was so pleasurable, she could barely breathe.

Slick with arousal, she whimpered and writhed at the feel of his calloused fingertip on her achingly sensitive nub. Her sweet spot clenched and pulsated with exquisite spasms. "Nick! Come inside me," she pleaded as he continued to stroke her with maddening finesse. "Please. I can't take anymore."

His dark head bent further as he kissed her navel. When his hot mouth lowered on her belly, she gripped his face and cried frantically, "No. I want you now."

He jerked his head up and met her eyes with a look so intensely aroused, all breath left her lungs. His fiery blue eyes held hers, glazed with passion and tortured with need. He spread her thighs and positioned himself between them. Primed to take her, his nostrils flared and the veins in his neck bulged as he braced his powerful body on his forearms and slid his hands under her buttocks, tilting her pelvis up to receive him. He kissed her neck before sliding his tongue inside her mouth and entering her at the same moment. She gasped as her tight entrance gave way to his voluptuous intrusion. Her womb convulsed with plea-sure-pain quivers as she adjusted to his size.

"Relax, baby. Take it all," he murmured hoarsely.

"Yes," she whimpered against his mouth, "please, Nick. More!" Her hands dug into his hard hips as he drove into her, his love-making demanding, explosive, utterly exquisite. Frantic, arcing desire catapulted her to a soaring crescendo. Her head thrashed from side to side, her limbs shook violently as her heart lurched and every sane thought left her mind. He was everything she wanted and more.

"That's it, baby. Give me everything," he growled, his voice gruff with need. "I want all of you." He surged inside her and her pelvis rose taking him in as deeply as she could. She clung to him whimpering and grasping and spiraling out of control under his driving thrusts until she came with a shattering cry, repeating his name over and over again.

Descending back to earth, she reveled in his deep, primal cry of release, a sound that filled her heart with joy. He buried his face in her neck. "Aah, Ronnie. So beautiful...so exquisite," he moaned, the sound rough and husky. "You're gonna be the death of me."

Blissful tears rolled down the sides of her face as she lay beneath his spent body, willing him not to move. She loved the weight of his strong body on hers, the possessive way he held her anchored to him. She ran her fingers through his damp, dark hair and kissed his temple as the tension left his body. With a low, satiated groan, he rolled to his side, taking her with him and cradling her to his chest. His strong arms wrapped around her protectively and held her firmly.

Love welled up inside Veronique over her complete oneness with Nick and the deep intimacy they'd shared. She had never felt happier...or more sated. The depth of her feelings for him was overwhelming and humbling.

After this, she'd never be the same.

They lay entwined together for a long, long time as fresh rain cleansed their naked bodies and the ocean breeze cooled their skin.

CHAPTER 13

*D*aisy waited until Nick's Land Rover was far enough down the dirt road, away from his house, before she left the thicket of pine trees. It was a stroke of good luck that he'd left and she could investigate what Veronique was about without him around.

She knocked on the door several times, surprised when Veronique didn't answer. She went around to the back of the house to check if she was in the patio. When she didn't find her there or in the back yard, she returned to the front and let herself in with her key.

She entered cautiously and the first thing she noticed was the stillness. Complete silence inside and no sign of Veronique. Could she be so lucky that the bitch was gone? After a thorough search, she went to Nick's bedroom and pulled down his bed linens. Leaning forward, she smelled the pillows. She inhaled deeply of the first one and smiled when Nick's masculine scent filled her hungry nostrils. She moved onto the other pillow and recoiled at the sweetly feminine scent of almonds. Her gut clenched with rage and jealousy. Just as she'd suspected—the loathsome bitch was already shacking up with Nick.

Daisy threw the pillow back on the bed and straightened the sheets with brisk, violent movements. Acid hatred burned a hole in her gut as she imagined them having sex. She searched the room for the bitch's things and when she didn't find any, she headed to the guest bedroom to snoop.

Entering the bedroom, she sneered when she saw Veronique's tank top and panties on the chair and her flip flops strewn on the floor. Her hair brush and toiletries were scattered on the desk beside a pad of paper and pens. She shook her head in disgust. The room had been perfectly tidy before Veronique's arrival, thanks to Daisy's meticulous housekeeping. A rich man like Nick deserved a perfect home, one kept beautifully by Daisy, not that messy bitch!

She turned her attention to Veronique's suitcase. Luckily, it was unlocked. Daisy flipped the top open and noticed everything inside was a jumble. She held up one sundress after another, scrutinizing every detail with a critical eye.

Nick paid her a generous salary, and she was saving most of it. She wished she could unload her son and have total freedom. Manolito was cute enough, but he was a lot of work and everyone expected her to be the perfect mother—which she wasn't. It had been a huge mistake getting pregnant so young and she was paying for it now. The constant guilt trip from Papi and the pressure from Manuel to marry her were driving her up the wall. She wished they'd butt out and leave her alone. She was at the top of her night classes, especially the computer ones, and her English was flawless, with no accent.

She had big plans.

One day she would not only be Nick's wife, but she'd be his right hand in everything. She had to convince Mami to take Manolito off her hands. She was better suited at caring for him anyway. She was only thirty-eight, and she loved pretending that Manolito was her own. She always said she wished she'd had a boy, so here was her chance. Let her enjoy him so Daisy could go after her goals without being shackled. The biggest obstacle was Manuel. He was a rutting bull with her and he constantly managed to get what he wanted. He didn't have to force her either. His rough moves always had her panting for more. *Damn him!*

Daisy sped up her actions as she rummaged through Veronique's suitcase. Underneath the clothes, she found several files of papers. When her hands dug further, she touched something hard and metallic. She pulled the object out of the suitcase and gave a silent whoop when she saw it was a digital camera. She quickly stashed it in her bag and opened one of the files. She rifled through the papers, reading as much as she could, her eyes widening at the startling information.

Pinpricks of excitement made her pulse race as she read about Nick's trial and learned his full name was Nicholas Cameron. *Daisy Cameron.* She tried the name on her lips and liked the sound of it. Instant wealth, instant power. She just needed to get rid of the bitch and restore Nick's need for *her* services. This time she'd lure him into bed and make sure he was a happy man. Men only needed sex and food to keep them satisfied, and she was an expert at both.

He was very generous with his money. If she played her cards right, she'd have a whole staff waiting on her hand and foot, and she'd work them hard.

A dose of black magic might get rid of the bitch. *Santería?* That was a thought...

She opened another file and read about a woman named Elizabeth Remington who was Nick's ex-wife. The tiny hairs on her nape lifted as she read more, realizing the golden egg she'd stumbled upon. She grabbed a marker from the desk and scribbled Elizabeth's name on her wrist for future reference. If she was going to win Nick over, she needed to know all about his ex.

She jumped when she heard Nick's car pull up the driveway. Crap! There wasn't enough time to check out his office. That was the only room in the house she wasn't allowed to clean. Situated on the second floor next to his gym, it overlooked the ocean. She could only imagine the view from up there because she'd never seen it. He always kept it locked with strict orders for her not to go in, which made her all the more curious.

When she heard a car door shut, she shoved the file back under Veronique's scrambled clothes where it had been with the other ones. Grabbing her bag, she ran out of the kitchen back door. Crouching at the back of the house, she hid behind the orange and red croton bushes as she watched Nick and Veronique.

He was shirtless and in faded jeans. Veronique wore his damp shirt—one that clung to her slim curves—and nothing else. Seething with jealousy, Daisy stared at the bitch, hating her with every cell in her body. Her stomach clenched when Veronique leaned forward to pick up her backpack from the trunk and Nick stroked her bare thighs with the hands of a man already familiar with her body. Veronique smiled up at him as he looped his arm over her shoulders and pulled her in for a lingering kiss.

Daisy inhaled sharply and turned away as bile rose in her throat. They'd had sex all right, she thought as bitter resentment and the urge for revenge seared her veins. She wanted Nick more than ever and she'd have him no matter what.

She would find a way to get rid of that bitch...even if she died trying.

CHAPTER 14

*O*ut of the blue that evening, Nick said, "I'm not planning on getting married again, Ronnie."

They had just finished eating dinner and Veronique was still in a euphoric daze after their lovemaking on the beach. Nick's blunt comment slapped her back to reality. She hadn't expected him to bring up the touchy subject so candidly, and for a moment she didn't know how to respond. She wasn't really surprised he felt that way, but it hurt that he felt compelled to tell her so she wouldn't get the wrong idea. Now that he'd had his fill of her, had he lost interest and come down to earth with a thud?

"How do you feel about that?" Nick said, not taking his eyes off her.

"It'll take more than that to drive me away, Nick," she said, her heart squeezing at the burden in his eyes. "Why do we have to talk about it now?"

"I want to be straight with you, Ronnie." He paused reflectively and then continued in a quiet tone. "I don't want to hurt you."

That hurt most of all. He was already pulling away from her, trying to dissuade her from becoming emotionally attached. "I'm a big girl. You don't have to protect my feelings," she said, harnessing her emotions as her confidence began to crumble.

He shook his head. "You're only twenty-eight, honey. You'll want more eventually. Marriage, children...all the stuff I've written off," he said wearily.

She put her finger over his lips. "Shh, don't say anymore. Please." She took a deep breath and tried to calm her anxious heart. She didn't want to see the concern in his eyes, the troubled emotions that made him doubtful. "Let's live in the moment. Pretend we're marooned on a deserted island," she urged, touching his arm.

"Can you really do that?" He sounded dubious, but his eyes held the barest glimmer of hope that made her heart lift. Would he agree to living in the moment too?

"Yes," she said fervently. "I want….I want to enjoy this time with you. Without a ticking clock. Without you getting all serious and practical-minded."

He remained silent, watching her intently.

"Today is almost over. We'll never have it again." She couldn't continue without her voice breaking. She swallowed against the thick emotion clogging her throat and tried to calm the hitch in her chest. She couldn't let him back away. Not now. Not ever, if she could help it, but she was willing to enjoy the present —for now.

He brushed a lock from her forehead. "You're wrong, Ronnie. We'll always have today."

Her heart soared. "Yes. You're right, Nick. Thank you," she said, wishing she could call him darling. She was timid about calling him endearments, even with the way he'd made love to her, fiercely, possessively, as if he couldn't get enough of her. He'd always been her darling, had been since she was a child. "I don't live in the past or the future. I live in the present. Let's take it one day at a time. Okay?" she asked, kissing the warm hollow behind his ear as she slowly glided her fingertip over the seam of his firm lips.

"Okay, baby," he said, his voice a sexy rumble in his chest. He kissed her finger and nipped at the fleshy pad of her fingertip. A tremor of exhilaration coursed through her. Ablaze with desire, she gave him a seductive smile that earned her a ride in his arms to the bedroom.

"I don't want to be a mood killer, but I'm not on the Pill," she said when he set her on her feet. Now *she* was being practical-minded, but it had to be said. Not that she didn't want to be pregnant with his child. Nothing would have made her happier, but she wouldn't do it to rope him in.

"No problem," he said smoothly. He unzipped his jeans and pulled them off.

"Aren't you worried we didn't use protection earlier?" she said, trying not to be distracted by the play of muscle and sinew as he reached for her.

"No. You won't be getting pregnant with me." His hands settled on her waist as he held her before him.

What did he mean by that? "What makes you so sure?"

"I always wanted to have children. My ex and I talked about it before getting married, but after a year of trying it didn't happen. All the medical tests came back that Elizabeth was fertile. She blamed me for not getting her pregnant."

"Were you ever tested?"

He gave a cynical shake of his head. "No, by then I had rethought starting a family. Elizabeth wasn't the same person I married. She became obsessed with wealth and power. It was an addiction."

"That bad?"

"Yeah. She spent longer hours working than I did." He gave a disgusted snort. "Yet in spite of all that, she didn't have a problem getting pregnant with Zack," he said, his tone harsh.

Veronique hadn't expected him to say that. "Oh. I'm sorry I brought it up."

"Don't be. I'm glad it's over," he said, gently squeezing her waist. "I haven't thought about Elizabeth in a long while. I'd rather think about you. Here," he said, removing her top and sliding her panties down her legs with a fluid motion. "With me." He smoothed his warm hands over her cool skin and backed her onto the bed. "Gorgeously naked," he added, his voice gravelly and aroused.

She lowered her body on the bed and when her back made contact with the sheets, she winced. "Ouch."

"What's wrong?" he said, pulling her into his arms. "You okay?"

"No, I mean yes. Well maybe," she said, wriggling against him.

He chuckled. "Which one is it?"

"All of the above. My skin feels a bit raw in some places. Especially my back."

"Let me take a look," he said. "Roll over."

"Hey, I'm not Baxter," she quipped, suddenly shy to lie before him naked and exposed in the waning daylight. Realizing it was silly to refuse, she turned over and clutched the pillow under her head.

"Relax." He blew softly on her flushed back and the cool air sent shivers skittering through her. "Poor baby. No wonder it's bothering you." He trailed tender kisses down her spine. "You're all pink and irritated from the sand and sea shells."

She craned her head to look behind her. "I am?"

"Yeah, mostly on your upper back and shoulders." He patted her bottom. "Good thing my hands protected the best part."

She shot him a quizzical look and his hands squeezed her buttocks in response.

She blushed at the amused sparkle in his eyes. "Oh, you mean when you held my... Um, never mind." She smiled at the delicious memory. "Yep, I was in good hands all right."

His smug smile was so sexy, she wanted to roll over and pull him in for a kiss, but his big hand was intimately pressed against the small of her back as the other hand reached for the pot of the honey almond cream she'd left on the nightstand. He leisurely smoothed it on her skin, starting at her neck, skimming the small indentation of her waist, over the crest of her bottom, the length of her legs down to her ankles. He took his time on each leg and then returned to her bottom and upper thighs, massaging them deeply until she was squirming and biting the pillow.

"I thought you said that part had been spared," she murmured with a muffled groan.

"Just making sure every inch gets pampered. Feel better now?"

"Mmmm, hmmm." Rosy-faced, she rolled over and fluffed her hair out on the pillow. Taking hold of his hand, she kissed the rugged back of it, and then turned it over to kiss the center of his hard palm. "You have wicked hot hands."

"For you," he said, his guttural voice promising a passionate night. He began to kiss her in earnest, his lips roving her curves and valleys as if she were the most succulent treat. The feel of his facial scruff grazing Veronique's skin made her toes curl and her pulse beat out of control.

"Your skin is so delicate, it's turning bright pink. Maybe I better shave." He stopped kissing her and rubbed his jaw.

"No, don't shave," she said huskily. "I like you that way."

The corners of his mouth turned up into a lazy grin as he reached for more cream. She'd never seen him smile like that— bad boy to the core. She caught her breath in anticipation of the night ahead.

Using the gentlest of strokes, his warm hands circled her breasts and lifted, plumping them upward and together. His thumb and forefingers tugged and squeezed her nipples with a deft touch that made her mindless with wanting him.

"Ohhh, Nick...Nick," she crooned, closing her eyes. His touch grew lighter, barely brushing her skin, teasing and tormenting until she could hardly bear it.

"So beautiful …your skin is so incredibly soft," he murmured hoarsely. He captured her mouth with plundering kisses as his questing hand roamed over the throbbing juncture of her thighs. "You taste good too. I'm gonna make love to you all night," he growled in her ear, his warm breath raising gooseflesh on her acutely sensitized skin.

Her eyes flew open and she licked her lips in anticipation. The pressure of his kisses had brought blood to the surface, making her mouth feel tender and engorged. Her pulse thrummed rampantly as she relived their fevered lovemaking on the beach. He'd been a masterful lover, drawing wild, uninhibited responses from her until she was limp with pure pleasure. A full night of that kind of intense, intimate bliss was almost inconceivable…

"All night," she repeated in a strangled voice, her thighs clenching and her pelvis bucking under the slippery caress of his fingers.

"Yes, baby," he said, taking her earlobe in his mouth. "All night. In every position. Until I get my fill of you."

He trailed voracious kisses down her neck and on her breasts, taking each nipple in his mouth for extra loving. The sweet rasp of his tongue made her sweet spot clench. Her stomach leapt as desire pooled inside her like lava, creating an internal blaze.

She wound her arms tightly around his neck and kissed the warm hollow of his throat, inhaling deeply of his heady scent. His prominent arousal pressed against her insistently, and she caressed the steely length of him.

"I'm yours, darling. All yours. Take me now," she whispered raggedly.

MUCH LATER, Nick rested his chin on Veronique's tousled hair.

They'd made love all night, learning each other's bodies. He'd taken his time, drawing out her pleasure, following up fiery climaxes with tender kisses. She'd returned the attention, pleasuring him until he was wrung out and satiated.

Sprawled on top of him, her head was tucked under his chin, her face resting on his chest. He loved the way her soft breasts and velvety nipples pressed against him and her knee nestled between his legs. Her throat purred with soft, contented sounds like a cuddly kitten.

Kissing the top of her head, he held her tight, delighting in the way her body hummed with aftershocks of their recent lovemaking. She'd matched his lust with fervor and a total lack of restraint. She'd been wild and magnificent—so beautiful and trusting.

How would it feel when his house was empty again? He didn't need to be alone and isolated anymore. He didn't want it either—he wanted her.

His life had been turned upside down with her arrival, especially when she'd told him, *"You're still that successful, self-made man, Nick. What I admire most is your integrity. Nobody can take that away from you unless you let them. I never believed a word of all that crap the media put out there."* Her loyalty had floored him then and it did now. They hadn't had any contact in the fifteen years since he'd last seen her, yet she'd never lost faith in him.

Maddening, irresistible and stubbornly loyal, she'd entrenched herself so deeply in his life that just thinking about her leaving gave him a cold, hollow ache in the pit of his stomach.

"Nick, tell me about your childhood," she said. "You mentioned your father had been a mean drunk. How mean was he?"

Nick shook his head. "I don't think you want to hear about it. It was ugly."

"Well, you already know about my disastrous childhood." She

smiled at him. "Look at us, we turned out all right in spite of it. Yours couldn't have been much worse than mine."

"Trust me, it was. I still have nightmares."

"About what?" Veronique kept her face tilted upward as she listened. "Tell me."

"As a kid, I never used to get a good night's sleep. I'd sleep fitfully until my father would get home and he was usually stinking drunk. Then the violence would begin. My old man would beat my mom viciously and if I tried to stop him, he'd whip me with his belt until his arm got tired. Then he'd finish up what he started with her." Nick shuddered as bile rose in his throat. He couldn't bring himself to mention the darkest part of his nightmares when his old man would kick and pummel his mom, leaving her in a crying heap on the floor.

"Oh, God," she moaned. "I'm so sorry, darling." Veronique cradled the side of his face and tenderly kissed his clenched jaw. "You don't have to say anymore if you don't want to."

He sucked in labored breaths. He couldn't believe he was sharing the vile memories of his childhood, the dark ones he never wanted to revisit. He hadn't told anyone about it, not even his ex-wife. Now that he'd started, he needed to finish.

"I used to climb into my baby sister's bed and cover her ears so she wouldn't hear the horror outside her bedroom door. No matter how I try to shake it, the awful sound of my mom weeping and desperately pleading is engraved in my mind. When I was eight, I told the school counselor about my dad and she helped my mom escape with me and my sister. The shelter we stayed in was for women hiding from their violent partners. Dad used to yell at us that he'd kill Mom if she ever left him."

She gave him a searching look. "How is your mom doing now? Is she okay?"

"Yeah, she had a hard life, but she's a survivor. As soon as I made enough money, I bought her a condo in a doorman building close enough so I could visit her. She always had a talent for painting, so she took art classes and has become an accomplished artist. It helped her heal."

"Oh, I'm so glad to hear that," Veronique said, hugging him.

"She deserves happiness after all the sacrifices she made to keep us fed and clothed. Her biggest fear was that my sister and I would end up in foster homes."

"What about your grandparents? Didn't they help her?"

"No. She was estranged from them. They were strict and very conservative. My mom was a sheltered only child and the one time she rebelled, she ended up pregnant and had to drop out of high school and get married. Her parents never accepted my dad. Ironically, they were right about him."

"She must be very strong."

"She is, and spiritual. When I was growing up, she always said, 'Remember whose child you are. I birthed you, but you're God's child. Use your talents to make a better world.'"

"I wish I could meet her," Veronique said. "Do you have any pictures of her?"

"I have some in my office. I'll show you tomorrow."

Ronnie was so different from Elizabeth. He'd mistakenly thought that marriage to the sophisticated Elizabeth Remington would somehow erase his tainted pedigree and give him a shot at a new life. Initially, she'd acted like she respected and liked his mom, but after many pretend illnesses and excuses not to visit her during the holidays, Nick realized something was off. It was during a fight when Elizabeth admitted her disdain for the blue-collar working class and included his mother in it, Nick decided the marriage was over. Good thing too because she was already hooking up with Zack.

"I think she'd like you," Nick said quietly.

"She must be so proud of you. I know I am. How did you cope?"

"Not very well as a kid. I felt powerless and sick to my stomach most of the time."

"Because you were afraid of your dad?"

"No, because I was afraid of what he'd do to my mom and my little sister. I had a constant knot of anguish in my stomach, ashamed that I was too scrawny to rescue her from the monster she'd married."

"But you did rescue her. You did the best thing a little boy could do. You went to your school counselor and got help—for all of you."

"I also worked my butt off to get as strong as steel, physically and mentally as I got older. If he ever threatened Mom again, he'd have to deal with me. Even with a restraining order, he was dangerous."

"Did he ever find you?"

"Yeah, when I was much older. He got wind of my success and tried to get money from me."

"How awful."

"He showed up drunk at the courthouse during the trial demanding money from my company. He was arrested when he pulled a knife on one of the reporters outside." He paused. "I'm sure you remember the circus that day. It was all over the news."

"Yes...I remember," she said softly. "Is he still in jail?"

"No, he died there of a heart attack." He scoffed, "Funny how that didn't constitute big news. I'm glad he died in jail. It's where he belonged." His gut twisted at the memory of the vast relief he'd felt at his old man's death. "I've done everything to disassociate myself from him. I legally changed my last name to my mom's maiden one, but that doesn't wipe out the bad seed I inherited."

"Don't ever say that again. You are *nothing* like your dad!" she cried passionately. "I have loved you from the first time I set eyes on you in camp."

"What?" Nick pulled back and stared at her incredulously. "You said you had a crush on me. That's not love." She had been nothing but a pest during camp and now she was telling him she'd loved him?

"It is to a little girl. Even as a kid, I appreciated how decent and honorable you were compared to the other counselors. You always went out of your way to help any of us kids who needed a hand."

"It was my job," he said quietly.

"No, it was more than that. You *care* about others." She nuzzled his neck with her face. "Earlier today you searched for me, worried about my safety. No one has ever shown that much concern for my welfare. You are the most heroic, most wonderful man I know, and I love you!" Tears sprung from her eyes, wetting his chest as she hugged him tightly. "It's true I used to have a girlish crush on you, but I'm not a little girl anymore. This is a woman's love," she said fiercely.

He caught her chin and tilted her face up. The look of pure love in her eyes made his insides clench and his heart ache. He raised her up to eye level, anchoring her beside him to gaze in her eyes.

"Ronnie," he said tenderly. "My brave, beautiful Ronnie."

Her eyes watered as they searched his with such profound hope, his heart rocked.

"I've treasured our time together...but..."

She froze in his arms, her eyes filled with alarm. "But what, Nick?"

"I don't want to hurt you. You know I don't intend to get married, and I—"

"Nick, I already told you. We're living in the moment. I know what I'm getting into. Don't take this away from me...from us!" She clutched his shoulders, her nails digging into his skin with desperation. "Don't regret this. I don't."

Nick didn't know what to say. He wished he could live up to Ronnie's absolute trust and confidence in him. She was special and unique, and she'd already carved a place in his heart, but he couldn't tell her he loved her back. It wasn't fair to mislead her. She would want more—marriage, children, the whole romantic picture.

Her soft hand circled his chest and settled over his heart. Pretty ironic, he thought ruefully. She already had his heart in the palm of her hand.

CHAPTER 15

When nobody answered the knock on Nick's front door, Daisy waited a few minutes and then let herself in. Stealthily, she made her way through the house, stopping to glance in each room. There was no sign of Nick or Veronique. As she approached Nick's bedroom, she noticed the door was open and she could hear the shower water running in the master bathroom. Tiptoeing closer, she heard sexual moans and intimate sounds of bodies and skin coming together.

Ugh, they were at it again.

With a sour twist of her mouth, she forced the insufferable image from her mind and concentrated on the hatred for Veronique mushrooming inside her. With a little luck, they'd stay in there a while longer and she could get her task done efficiently. She ran to the guest bedroom and threw open Veronique's suitcase. Pushing aside the pile of clothes, she put Veronique's camera in and covered it with clothes, just the way she'd found it yesterday. Good thing she had a photographic memory because she'd memorized the top articles of clothing and where they'd been in the suitcase. It looked as if the bitch hadn't touched anything since their return from the beach. Hopefully, she hadn't noticed her camera missing.

Daisy took one more look around the room and left. She crept down the hall and glowered when she passed the master bedroom and heard their voices coming from the bathroom. They were going to be in for a big surprise, one they'd never expect. She felt like kicking the door down, but she darted away before they came out.

Just as she cautiously closed the back kitchen door, she heard a rustling sound behind her.

"Where are you going?" Felipe asked. "I thought you were cleaning today."

Daisy jumped and whirled around to face her nosy father. "I'm going back to Fort Myers with Manuel. Those two are busy." She rolled her eyes. "It's obvious they don't need me around."

Felipe nodded.

"Papi, don't tell them I came by. They'll know I caught them in the shower," she said, hiding her rage with a cunning smile. "They were going at it like—"

"Be quiet." Felipe's stern eyes tried to silence her. "Stay out of their business, Daisy. They are in love."

"No they're not! He's bonking the bitch, that's all," she huffed.

"Don't talk like a slut!"

Daisy clamped her mouth shut so tightly, her teeth hurt. She wanted to lash out and scream obscenities at her father, but she couldn't risk unleashing his temper, especially in Nick's yard. Instead of telling him to go to hell, she gave him a hate stare.

"When are you going to pick up Manolito?" he asked wearily.

"He's staying with Mami for the rest of the week," she said, narrowing her eyes at him aggressively. She wasn't about to let him guilt her into picking up the kid. She had something better to do, especially now. It was going to be difficult to get rid of Veronique since she'd wormed her way into Nick's home...and pants. How long was the bitch planning to camp out at his house —forever?

The need for revenge exploded inside Daisy. After hearing them in the shower, she wanted to annihilate the bitch for good. She was done waiting. Now that the roads had been cleared and power was back in Fort Myers, she could set her plan in motion.

Felipe shook his head, his eyes severe with condemnation. "Suit yourself," he said, turning away from her.

"I will." He didn't know the half of it. If everything worked out, she'd be sitting pretty in Nick's mansion telling *him* what to do!

Peasant.

CHAPTER 16

The next couple of days rolled by hot and sultry as Nick and Ronnie swam in the ocean, fished together, ate together and slept together. Nick made love to her as often and as long as he wanted and she was always wildly passionate, returning his hot caresses with her own. He got to know a side of Ronnie he'd never imagined. Underneath the intrepid journalist, lay a young woman who had constantly put herself in danger physically, but had always guarded her heart. She'd candidly told him she hadn't had luck in love, until now.

One morning while Ronnie got ready for the day, Nick went outside and met with Felipe, who'd promised to come by early.

"Morning, Felipe. How's the family?" Nick asked, clapping him on the back.

"Doing good. How is your lady friend?" Felipe gave him a smile of male camaraderie. "She's very pretty."

"Thanks, I'll tell her you said so," Nick said, smiling back. He wondered where Daisy was. She hadn't been by since the day after the hurricane, and that wasn't like her. "Is Daisy's son still sick?"

"No, Manolito's fine now. And he's getting bigger every day." Felipe beamed with pride.

"Good. Where's Daisy? I haven't seen her since the day after the hurricane."

Felipe's smile vanished. "She's with Manuel. She was planning on going to Fort Myers, but if you need her, I'll tell her to come here instead." He looked uncomfortable as he rubbed the back of his neck and shifted his stance.

"No, don't tell her to come. The house is clean and picked up. I was just wondering."

Felipe nodded.

"There are lots of fruits and vegetables left over from the hurricane. Take as much as you want for your family and friends," Nick said.

"Gracias," Felipe said, thanking him.

The two of them worked most of the morning hauling big bags of fallen fruit and vegetables to Felipe's truck. Nick had just handed Felipe the last one to load, when he heard a scream that sounded like "Nooo!" coming from behind him.

He swiveled around and caught sight of Ronnie on the front porch. His heart in his throat, he sprinted to the house and bounded up the steps.

Slumped against the wall, Ronnie clutched her cell phone to her heart. "Oh God, oh God," she repeated tremulously, her cell phone slipping from her hands.

Nick caught the phone in time and slid it into his shorts' pocket. "What's wrong?" He raised her chin with his thumb and saw all the color had drained from her face, leaving it alarmingly pale. Seconds ticked by like hours as he waited for her to form words through trembling lips.

"Slinky is gone."

The wide-eyed shock in her eyes shook him to the core. "Who is Slinky?"

Veronique swallowed a few times before she spoke. "She was my cat...my *baby*," she whispered, her eyes brimming with tears.

He squeezed her shoulders gently and peered into her eyes, jolted by how eerie they looked. Why was she so frightened?

"Did she run away?" he asked gently.

"No. She's dead. Gone forever." Her raw voice sounded so despondent it tore at his heart.

"Oh, I'm sorry, honey," he said, putting his arm around her bent shoulders.

Her head hung forward as she wrung her hands. "I never had a pet before her. Maman said animals were dirty and wouldn't let them in the house," she said in a small voice. "I always wanted a pet, but it was impossible with all the traveling."

He heard the pain in her heart and wished he could make it vanish.

"Slinky was everything I'd ever dreamed of. A fluffy white ragdoll kitty who stole my heart the minute I laid eyes on her." She gazed at him with desperate, stricken eyes. "It's my fault she died. I wasn't there to protect her."

Nick's brows snapped together. He hadn't expected her to say that. Sadness over the loss of her pet was understandable, but guilt?

"Your fault? That's nonsense. How did you find out?"

"I finally got through to Natasha." She squeezed her eyes shut and pressed her fingers to her temples, massaging them in small circles.

"What did she say?" He rubbed the length of her spine with gentle, soothing strokes.

She stared at him as if in a trance, her eyes hazy and wide with shock. "I can't bear to say it out loud."

From afar, Nick caught sight of Felipe's alarmed look and upturned hands. He shook his head and waved him away.

Turning his attention back to Ronnie, he said, "Let's go inside." He kept his arm around her quaking shoulders as he led her into the house and shut the door. "Now, tell me what Natasha said."

"Somebody killed Slinky. It was sick, cruel…" Her voice broke and she looked close to passing out. "I can't wrap my head around that kind of viciousness."

Black fury formed a block of cement in his chest at the thought of anyone harming her. He cradled her to him, troubled by how fragile and broken she felt in his arms, as if she might fall apart at any moment. "Breathe slowly and try to calm your heart rate," he murmured against her temple.

Veronique leaned her forehead on his shoulder and drew in harrowing breaths.

After a few moments, he said, "Okay, honey. Try to tell me what happened."

She heaved a ragged sigh and looked up at him helplessly. "Slinky died of a broken neck. Snapped in two."

"How did it happen?"

"The vet thinks she was strangled." She turned her face into his chest and moaned.

Nick's gut constricted. *Who in holy hell would strangle a cat?* An icy stab of alarm made him pull her closer, securely sheltering her in his arms.

"I'm sorry, baby. If it wasn't for this damn hurricane I'd buy you a kitten." Instead of comforting her, his words unleashed a torrent of sobs. He held her tight, patted her back and let her cry it out as he struggled with mounting impatience. He knew she needed to calm down before she could continue, but a sick feeling crawled under his skin when he contemplated the reasons anyone would strangle her cat. There was a clear threat there.

After several hiccupping snuffles, she said, "Slinky was a starving kitten when I rescued her last winter. She had gotten separated from her mother during a snowstorm. This may sound stupid, but sometimes it felt like she was the only family I had." Her voice quavered with sorrow. "I loved her so much."

"I'm sure you did," he murmured, resting his chin on top of her head.

She clung to him, her arms wrapped tightly around his waist as she sighed heavily. A few moments later, she wiped her eyes and touched his wet chest. "I'm sorry. I need a tissue badly."

"It's okay." Nick kissed her forehead and released her. "Be right back."

VERONIQUE WIPED her eyes and took calming breaths as she watched Nick's retreating back. Dread mushroomed inside of her, adding to her misery. She was grateful for his kindness, and touched when he'd kissed her forehead so tenderly, but she wasn't ready to disclose details of her investigation and its possible link to Slinky's death.

She sank down on the sofa with her head in her hands. This was *awful*. Natasha had barely gotten the words out about Slinky before bursting into tears. She felt bad for Tash and was worried about her safety. She'd told her to leave the studio apartment immediately and be extra cautious about watching her back.

Nick returned with a box of tissues and joined her on the couch. He handed her a tissue and patted her knee.

"Thanks." Veronique dried her eyes and blew her nose.

"Tell me everything Natasha said. Start from the beginning," he said in a compelling tone.

Veronique got up and paced the room. She didn't feel like repeating everything, but Nick was concerned. He deserved to know. "She said she got home late and found Slinky lifelessly on the floor."

Nick's face was stone hard as he watched her. She had to look away to pull herself together.

"Ronnie." The tension in his voice drew her attention back to him. "Was there any sign of a break-in?"

"I don't know. I was too upset to think of asking."

"Did they steal anything?"

"I'm not sure. I feel like an idiot." Her mouth twisted with self-deprecation. "Some reporter I am. Something horrible happens and I don't even ask the right questions."

"You were in shock," he told her kindly.

Veronique nodded and took a deep breath. "Natasha didn't mention how they got in or if they took anything of value. She said everything looked untouched...except for Slinky." She stopped before him and put her closed fist against her mouth, wishing she didn't have to continue.

"What else did she say?"

"There was a note left behind."

Nick's dark brows furrowed over narrowed eyes. "What was on it?"

Veronique cringed inwardly as she forced her voice to sound steady. "It said, 'you're next." A fine sheen of cold sweat made her shiver and rub her arms.

Nick shot up and took hold of her elbow. "Ronnie, you need to come clean with me. What's going on?" he demanded. His tone was taut with restraint and she wondered at what point he'd lose patience.

"Okay, just don't get your shorts in a bunch when I tell you." Veronique took a deep breath and expelled it forcefully. "Somebody fired a shot at me in a Miami hotel parking lot on the morning before I drove over here."

He froze. "What! Are you telling me a sniper almost hit you?"

Veronique pinched the bridge of her nose with her thumb and forefinger and closed her eyes briefly. "Yeah."

"Did you call the police?" Nick demanded.

"Of course. I spent over two hours at the station, but in the end they weren't much help. They told me to be extra careful and report any other threat to my safety."

"That's it?" he asked incredulously.

"Yes, that was the extent of it."

"That doesn't make sense. Since when do Miami police take a sniper lightly?" He stared at her with questioning eyes.

"I don't know," she said, frustrated. "Random shootings happen in a big, cosmopolitan city like Miami."

"That wasn't random. Who is targeting you?" His unwavering gaze held her rooted to the spot.

"I'm not sure," she hedged.

"You're not sure? That means you have an idea," he said, his gaze so forceful she averted her eyes and resumed pacing.

"Look at me."

A quiet command in a strained voice. Veronique stopped in her tracks and turned slowly to meet his eyes. It was hard not to squirm under his piercing gaze. Blue fire blazed in his eyes as he caught her chin and pinned her with a gripping look.

"Ronnie."

"I need to get back to New York today." She hated to leave him, but given this new development, she had to.

"Hell no. You're not leaving," he said emphatically.

Hope blossomed at the change in him, despite the dire circumstances. When she'd first shown up, Nick had wanted to get rid of her ASAP and now he wouldn't let her leave. If it hadn't been for Slinky's murder, she'd have been ecstatic.

"You're asking me not to go?"

"Damn right. I'm *telling* you not to," he said tersely.

She met his gaze and her heartbeat faltered the moment she saw his face was set in grave lines. His eyes glittered with suspicion and his shadowed jaw ticked rhythmically as he stared at her for a long, long time.

"It's obvious you're a target. Are you investigating someone who might want to harm you?" he asked.

She shook her head and averted her gaze again. She couldn't meet his probing eyes, not when she was keeping information from him. Nervous tension coiled inside her, making her nauseated and jittery. She hated lying to Nick by omission, but she had to. She couldn't divulge anything about what she was investigating until she had the final piece of solid evidence.

"You better not be lying to me." He drew in a heavy sigh and shook his head. "We'll discuss this later when you're feeling better," he said and walked out, his stride measured.

CHAPTER 17

$\mathcal{V}$eronique flinched at his departing tone. It felt wrong not to come clean with Nick, but as much as she wanted to, she couldn't. Not yet.

She hugged herself, heartened that she and Nick had reached a new level of intimacy. She still couldn't believe it. All these years she'd thought about him, yearning to connect as an adult, but never finding the right moment. When her career had taken off as a news reporter, she'd planned on seeking him out, but it was too late by then. He was already engaged to Elizabeth. Fred had broken the news to her gently, knowing her devotion to all things Nick. She'd followed his career with such pride, hoping someday she'd get a chance to tell him so.

Last night while he hadn't told her he loved her back, he had made exquisite love to her. She would take that. He'd also been incredibly open about his childhood traumas and the deep-rooted shame of having a brutal, alcoholic father. She'd felt humbled and closer to him than ever. Hearing the anguish in his voice, she had desperately wanted to wipe away his traumatic childhood. He'd needed to expose the ugly part of his background, to see if she'd still be around in the morning. Little did he know how much she adored him. The protective, compassionate side of Nick made him all the more heroic and she loved him madly for it.

To lift her spirits she allowed herself a dream. Someday, somehow, they'd have a family of their own. He would make an awesome dad—one that his kids would adore and be proud of. She would hold onto that dream for some sort of consolation.

She still couldn't believe or accept the awful news about Slinky. Her heart constricted in a vise of misery over her sweet kitty's slaying, especially since there was nothing she could do about it. It was final—and so unfair. She wouldn't be able to get another pet, especially if she didn't know where she'd be in the next six months.

She'd probably never deliver the story on Nick she'd hoped would revive her career. She wouldn't unless Nick was in agreement, which was a stretch at best. After he'd bared his soul to her last night, revealing his difficult childhood dealing with an abusive, drunk father and how ferociously he'd tried to protect his mom and sister, she respected his right to privacy. Out of allegiance to him, she'd fervently wanted to tell his side of the story, but she'd never do anything to hurt him. Ever.

Her life would never be the same. She suddenly craved having a home with Nick, having his baby and another kitty like Slinky. She wanted all of those things so badly it scared her. Why did it have to feel impossible and unattainable? *Because you want Nick,* she told herself morosely. She shouldn't have told him that she didn't care if they ever got married. She'd only said it so he would stop trying to push her away emotionally. Their physical connection was so in sync it made her ecstatic.

What would it take for him to hold her dear to his heart, to believe he couldn't live without her? That's how she felt about him. In spite of his rigid control and initial demands to be left alone, it hadn't crushed his inherent warmth. Nick was a hot-blooded, generous lover and she couldn't bear to imagine going back to their previous impasse. She couldn't allow him to retreat to his reclusive life before he had a chance to fall in love with her. She loved him, but she had no idea if his desire for her would turn into love. She might never find out if she left. It was too disheartening to consider.

The need to wrap up her investigation ASAP was so pressing her hands shook with impatience as she rummaged through her suitcase and pulled out the files at the bottom. Studying the stark evidence in front of her renewed her determination to expose Elizabeth Remington's illegal dealings. After the trial, Nick's partner, Zack, had been convicted to two years in the federal penitentiary, but Elizabeth had escaped unscathed. Justice had been served when Nick was exonerated from the charges, but not his ex-wife—she was guilty as all hell. Veronique was sure of it.

She had started investigating Elizabeth when the trial ended. She'd flown to Nick's home state of North Carolina and interviewed two high schools funded through his foundation. Both were success stories, rich in funds for the arts and computer sciences, and bourgeoning with sports programs.

But the third school funded by the foundation in Haiti was a disaster. The *École des Jeunes Travailleurs*, which translated to School of Young Laborers, was impoverished with tattered books, virtually no school supplies, substandard food and no computer literacy programs. The principal, Pierre Morais, was thankful for the little they'd received, but clearly he hadn't gotten enough money to fulfill the original development plan after the initial deposit from the Cameron Hope Foundation. When she mentioned the scholarship recipients, he acted surprised and said it was the first he'd heard of any scholarships. She didn't know whether to believe him or not. Disgusted, she'd turned away, not wanting to reveal her suspicion of corruption until she had sufficient evidence.

Digging deeper, Veronique discovered that an offshore trust company in Grand Cayman handled funding for the non-U.S.

activities of the Cameron Hope Foundation. At first no one in the firm would meet with her, let alone answer her questions, until one of the assistants, a twenty-two-year-old girl named Maya, contacted her to meet at the hotel. Maya told her she was quitting her job and moving to the U.S. to marry a Marine. She wanted to set the record straight that she'd had no involvement in Elizabeth's dealings, that she'd only *seen* records of money going into an account in Macau—China of all places. On the condition of anonymity, she'd handed over a paper trail of PDF documents and money transfers from Grand Cayman to Macau.

Veronique had a file full of evidence that a big part of the money supposedly going to *École des Jeunes Travailleurs* in Haiti was going through Grand Cayman, and through a cleverly designed arrangement, was being fraudulently funneled onto Macau. She had copies of bogus invoices, sub-account bank statements corresponding to *École des Jeunes Travailleurs* and copies of transfer confirmations to Alfa Bank of Macau.

She just needed the original payment instructions signed by Elizabeth authorizing the trust company to execute the monthly transfers. Veronique couldn't wait to get her hands on the documents from Maya.

Anxious to get everything tied up and share the information with Nick, she dialed Maya's number from her personal cell phone, not her work one, but the call went straight to voicemail. Preferring not to leave a message, she tried again several times.

When someone finally answered in the late afternoon, she was surprised to hear a male voice.

"May I speak to Maya?" she asked, deepening her voice.

"She's not here." The man's tone was curt and his island accent heavy.

"Who am I speaking with?"

"This is Will, Maya's brother. Who's this?" He sounded suspicious.

"It's Veronique, a friend of hers. When do you expect Maya to return?"

"I dunno. She left Grand Cayman three days ago and hasn't been in touch." His voice sounded strained.

A tremor of unease made her grip the phone tightly. Maya had told her she'd leave for the States in a week. Something—or someone—must have compelled her to leave earlier.

"Have you spoken to her in the past three days?" Will asked, bringing Veronique back to the present.

"No, we haven't been in touch in a week. Did she leave a note?" she asked cautiously.

"No. She took all her stuff and left. The only thing she forgot was her phone."

"Oh." She paused. "If she gets in touch with you, please tell her to call Veronique. She has my number."

"I have it too now," Will replied in a way that gave her pause. Was that a subtle threat? She hung up before he could make more comments or ask questions.

Veronique immediately called Eric, the fact-checker who'd worked with her on many cases before losing his job with the station. They'd stayed in touch since then and he often said he owed her big time for the mistake that got him fired and her demoted. It was time to collect on his promises to do right by her.

When the call went to voicemail, Veronique said, "Eric, please call me back. I don't want to use up my battery, so I'll make this quick. See if you can find out the whereabouts of a girl named Maya Magnus. She works in Grand Cayman." She heard the beep of another call coming in. "Never mind, I need to take this call. I'll text if I need you," she said and clicked in to the call. She was relieved to hear Maya's voice.

"Maya! I was so worried about you. Where are you?" Veronique asked.

"I'm staying with my brother, Will. He has a studio in downtown Miami."

"I'm glad you're okay. I was worried about you." She breathed a huge sigh of relief. Knowing Maya was safe and out of Grand Cayman eased the anxious knot in her stomach.

"Will is fielding my calls. The office has been calling me nonstop since I quit."

"I can imagine. How did they react to your resignation?"

"They didn't have much choice. I reminded the higher ups that I'd been complaining about my boss, Philip's sexual harassment for months and it was intolerable. They know they haven't done anything about it."

"I'm glad you're out of there. Do you have what I need?"

"Yes. I'm leaving to visit my boyfriend in Virginia, but I'll be back in Miami next Monday."

Shoot, another week to wait. "Please be extra careful."

"I'm not worried. My brother's tough. So is Frank."

Frank was Maya's Marine fiancé, and Veronique had no doubt he was tough. "Glad to hear it. Text me your brother's address and I'll contact you as soon as I can get there."

"Okay." She jotted the address in her notebook as soon as Maya texted it. Her spirits lifted the minute she hung up. It was time to tell Nick everything.

CHAPTER 18

$\mathcal{N}$ick was so furious that Ronnie hadn't told him about the gunshot until now, that he went for a jog along the shoreline to calm down. When he returned, he concentrated on cleaning the pool, scrubbing the interior, skimming the water with a net for stray leaves and adding chemicals to balance the Ph level.

He tried to put his frustration and anger aside. He knew Ronnie was hurting over her cat's killing, but she was in danger and damned well better open up and tell him what was going on. He'd get his answers tonight.

On his way to his bedroom, he caught a glimpse of Ronnie in the kitchen. She turned when he called her name.

"Hey you," she said, smiling. "Dinner's almost ready. Want to eat early?"

He was surprised at how much her mood had lightened since this morning. "Sure. Keep it warm. I'm gonna shower first," he said and headed toward the bathroom.

The blast of frigid water was just what Nick needed to cool off as he showered and washed the sweat from his skin and scalp. But the jet stream did nothing to clear Ronnie from his overheated mind…and body. She'd looked tantalizing just now with her hair up in a ponytail, baring her nape and revealing her soft, creamy skin. He couldn't wait to bury himself again in her wild, sweet essence. He closed his eyes and willed his body not to react. Too late. He was already hard. It was innate, organic, the way he responded to her. She had an uncanny ability to command his attention and distract him from everything but her when they were together.

Freshly showered and wearing a loose cotton shirt and khaki shorts, he went to the kitchen only to find it empty. Barefoot, he headed down the hall in search of Veronique.

"Ronnie? Where are you?" he called out.

"Out here, Nick," she answered. "We're having a picnic on the porch."

He found her sitting on the top step of the veranda beside a tray of food. Her glossy hair was no longer in a ponytail, but tousled about her bare shoulders. He eased down beside her, careful not to knock over the candles on the tray.

"Nice touch. Looks festive." For someone who claimed not to be domestic, she'd done a fine job with the picnic, adding wine and candles. What was all this about? Her eyes sparkled with eagerness, like she was bursting to tell him something. She looked far different from the broken girl who'd sobbed in his arms earlier. It was good to have the old Ronnie back.

She smiled. "Thanks, but I can't take the credit for the food. I heated up two of Daisy's meals again. The frozen food won't stay frozen much longer, so we might as well eat hearty," she said, handing him a plate of food.

"What are we having?"

"I think it's beef stew. Smells good, doesn't it?"

"Tastes good too. Daisy calls it *boliche*," he said, between mouthfuls.

"Where's Baxter?"

"He left with Felipe."

"Oh, too bad. I miss him." Veronique's sudden wistful tone showed she was thinking of Slinky, but he didn't bring up her cat. She needed to heal and block the memory of the vicious way her pet had been killed.

They lapsed into silence as Nick devoured the meal. He was ravenous after working straight through lunch, only stopping to drink water and stay hydrated.

When they finished eating, Ronnie put everything back on the tray, pushed it away and scooted closer to him until her soft arm rested against his. If she knew how much a mere brush of her skin affected him, she didn't let on. She was too intent on looking up at the darkening sky and oblivious to the fine mist of rain descending on them.

"It's going to be a beautiful night," she said softly. "Will you stay with me here for a while?" She turned to him with expectant eyes.

"Sure. If you don't mind the rain, I don't."

"I don't mind. As I recall, you don't either," she said huskily.

Nick draped an arm around her shoulders and pulled her in close. She sighed as she rested her head on his shoulder. "Still feeling blue?" he asked, tilting her chin to peer into her eyes.

"A bit. I don't normally dwell on stuff, but I'm blindsided by what happened to Slinky."

"That's understandable, honey." He stroked her silken hair from her face and kissed her temple. She smelled of flowers and rain, an intoxicating combination that made him want to bury his face in her hair.

Dusk enveloped them and the light rain stopped, clearing the skies of clouds and ushering in glittery stars and a slim, crescent moon.

"How do *you* feel, Nick?" she asked, pulling away to gaze in his eyes.

"About what?" Was she asking how he felt about her?

Her unwavering gaze held his. "Everything. The trial, your ex-wife…"

"Where's that coming from?" He'd shared plenty with her last night. This wasn't the moment to bring up the disastrous past year. Not when the pearly twilight bathed her in a luminous glow, making him want to take her inside for more loving.

"I want to know where you stand on certain things."

"You've had enough grief today without adding mine. I've been betrayed one time too many. I don't care to rehash it," he said. "End of subject."

"What do you mean end of subject?" Her eyes clouded with hurt. "I'd never do anything to betray your confidence, Nick. Surely, you know that."

Her solemn tone tugged at his heart, but he remained silent. He'd heard plenty of assurances like that from Elizabeth who had often said, "Nick, I'm your best ally. Together, we're brilliant. I'll always be your champion." Look where that had landed him—he'd damn near ended up in the state penitentiary serving time for something he hadn't done.

But this was Ronnie, not Elizabeth. As she sat before him, her heart and soul shining in her wondrous eyes, his heart rose in his throat clogging it with emotion.

"I believe you," he said gruffly. "Happy now?"

"More than you can ever imagine," she said, hugging him around the waist. She wasn't going to let it go at that, he realized, when she searched his eyes, her chin lifted at a stubborn angle. "What do you want most in life?"

"That's a loaded question. What do *you* want most?"

"Professionally or personally?"

"Let's start with professionally."

"More than anything, I want to restore my reputation as a first class journalist," she said without hesitation. Her eyes burned with determination and he could just imagine her fervor and dedication to every case she reported.

"Fair enough. And personally?"

She clasped her hands around her knees and leaned her head back to gaze at the stars in the horizon. Her face grew somber as she gathered her thoughts. She looked vulnerable, hesitant to divulge her feelings. That was a first. Ronnie's feelings were usually laid out in the open for everyone to see, especially him.

"Actually…" She hesitated and smiled. "I've been thinking about it a lot lately. This might sound lame because I love to roam free, being the first to break a story wide open. That gives me a real high."

"Nothing wrong with that, Ronnie. It's who you are."

"Exactly, but I haven't finished telling you how I feel. I used to get restless and always want to be on the go. But after this week, I've realized how lonely I've been. There's been something missing." She paused and looked up at the sky. "All of a sudden I want a place to call home. My studio is just my landing pad between assignments. I rent it furnished and I still have stuff in boxes from my last move." She studied the stars as she spoke softly, keeping her gaze from connecting with his.

"Why haven't you unpacked?"

She shrugged. "Part procrastination and part not knowing where I really want to be. I'm subletting the place for six months, and then I have to move on."

"Where would you want to live?"

"I'm not sure. I have a lot of decisions to make," she said, gazing at him with questing eyes.

"I've been thinking about where I want to go from here too," he admitted. "But this place has grown on me."

She sighed and her eyes turned dreamy. "I can see why. It's truly paradise with the turquoise waters and all that glorious white sand. Even the sunsets are magical with their pink and purple hues."

"Yeah, it's beautiful and there aren't a lot of people to deal with," he said. "You've seen the island before and after the hurricane hit. That doesn't give you an idea of how peaceful it usually is."

"True, but you can't stay away from civilization forever…can you?" The profound expectation in her eyes rattled him.

She had a point. Before she had come, he hadn't been able to stand being around people. Now he was dreading her departure. He'd grown accustomed to having her there, especially tonight when she smelled like an angel and all he could think about was burying himself inside her tight, velvety warmth. He'd never get his fill of her. She didn't only bring him sexual pleasure—she made him feel alive.

"Nick?" she prodded.

"I plan to get back in the saddle and take the helm again at my foundation. I was expelled from it when I was indicted on insider trading charges."

"You were chairman of the board, right?"

"Yes." His mouth twisted. "Ironic isn't it? Zack's in jail and I'm no longer CEO because my name might tarnish my own foundation," he said, disgusted at the paradox.

"Who runs the show now?"

"My ex-wife is the president, always has been. When we started the foundation, Elizabeth ran it full time while I worked and traveled. She serves under the direction of the executive board. Out of five board members, we're down to three." *But not for long*, he thought darkly. She was garnering public goodwill with her philanthropy, and buying time until Zack got out of jail.

"Is Fred one of them?"

"No. He used to be the secretary until I got kicked off. Then he quit."

"So you only have three board members now?"

"Yeah, there's Elizabeth's family lawyer, Ron Comptel, and Pete Gershon, a college friend of ours. Pete's a major party animal. He's only on the board to boost his public image. He couldn't care less about the fund, but as long as he continues to bring in big funds, we keep him on."

"Hmm. One of those," she said, her mouth pressed with censure.

Nick nodded. "Pete donates money. Ron, the lawyer, collects his fees for not doing much, and they all let Elizabeth run the show."

"Are you okay with that?"

"Hell no. I don't trust Elizabeth. Or anyone in my prior life," he added with a cynical curl of his lips.

"What are you going to do about it?" she challenged, her tone sharper than usual.

"The foundation is in my name. It was my brainchild and I plan to regain control."

"Good." She surprised him by giving his thigh a hearty slap. "That's the best thing I've heard all day."

"Why does that please you so much?" He took hold of her hand, struck by how strongly she squeezed his hand.

"I want you to be happy," she said exuberantly, and kissed his jaw. "That's why."

Nick wound his hand in her silky hair and kissed her. Her mouth went soft and pliable beneath his, her lips parting and taking in his tongue with a soft little moan.

"I want you to be happy too. *Very* happy," he drawled, insatiable for more of her sweet surrender. "Let's go for a swim." He tugged her hand as he rose from the steps. "The pool is sparkling clean and warm."

"Sounds tempting, but not yet," she demurred.

"I thought you'd be all for a skinny dip," he said, sounding disappointed.

"Of course I am, but not yet." Veronique squeezed his hand and gazed at him with anxious eyes, praying that the trust he'd professed didn't vanish over what she was about to tell him.

His brows knitted together in puzzlement. "What's wrong, honey? You look white as a ghost."

"I have something to tell you. It's important information." Her heart thudded painfully in her chest when she saw his smile fade and his features sharpen with suspicion.

He sank down beside her, his large body landing with a thud. "What is it?"

She took a deep, calming breath. "It has to do with your foundation."

"What about it?"

"Please listen to me and don't get mad." This was the dreaded make or break moment. If she could only get him to hear her out, he'd understand why she hadn't told him earlier.

"Why would I get mad?" he asked, removing his hand from hers. He already looked troubled; she could only imagine his reaction when she filled him in on everything.

"I've been investigating your ex-wife."

Nick's dark brows snapped together. "Elizabeth?" He paused and drew in a sharp breath. "Why?"

"All during your trial, I wanted to reach out to you because I knew you'd been wronged. Then when I found out where you were, I started investigating the trial and everything related to your foundation."

"What does this have to do with Elizabeth?"

"Something didn't add up when only Zack was sent to jail. I believed you were innocent all along, but I had strong reservations about Elizabeth. That's when I decided to investigate her activities." Her words came rushing out as she stared at the transformation in him.

Nick's skin was stretched tight over his sharp cheekbones, his jaw clenched, his mouth set as he stared at her with severe blue eyes. Anger reverberated in shock waves from his body. "Elizabeth is dead to me. She betrayed me more than you can ever imagine. Don't mention her again," he said vehemently before he got up and turned away.

She shot up and grabbed his forearm. "Don't turn away from me! Stay and listen to what I have to tell you." Her body shook with exasperation as she faced him, trying to get a grip on her temper. "Elizabeth is still screwing you over, Nick. She's syphoning money from your foundation and sending it to an undisclosed account in Macau."

He went as still as marble. The only thing moving in his rigid body was a ticking muscle in his jaw. His eyes targeted her like blue lasers.

"What are you talking about?" he said in a deceptively soft voice.

"Elizabeth gave instructions for funds transfers to two schools in North Carolina, but not all the money that was supposed to go to the *École des Jeunes Travailleurs* in Haiti got there. Only a small portion of it."

"How much snooping did you do to find this out?" His voice was unnerving as he stared at her.

She thrust her shoulders back and narrowed her eyes at him. She was so anxious for Nick to trust her, she was beyond letting his caustic comments hurt her. Naturally, he would lash out. He had to be in shock over what she'd divulged, incensed at her for meddling in his affairs, and most likely furious with himself for not suspecting Elizabeth. She understood how he felt. Her initial reaction to the evidence had been a bone-chilling urge to hunt Elizabeth and take her down.

"Well?" he said, not taking his eyes off her.

She took a deep breath, filling her lungs with much-needed oxygen as she prepared for his interrogation. "I went to visit all three schools. The ones in North Carolina were thriving, but the one in Haiti was a disaster. The place is barely running with minimum resources. Pierre Morais, the director—"

"I know who the director is," he said curtly.

"Yes, of course you do. Mr. Morais told me the school got very little support from the Cameron Hope Foundation. He also had no idea what I was talking about when I mentioned the scholarships. That's when I began to suspect that the money was being sent elsewhere."

"What evidence do you have?"

"I have a paper trail that incriminates Elizabeth from the trust company she used in Grand Cayman to the bank account in Macau."

"Where's the paper trail? In New York?"

"No. It's here. I have hard copies of everything."

"Here?" He stared at her incredulously. "You've been sitting on this information since you got here and you waited until now to tell me. Why?" he demanded, accusation sharp in his voice.

"I couldn't do it before, Nick. I was waiting for one more document before I could tell you."

"And now you have the document? How is that possible?"

"I don't have it in my hands yet. I'm supposed to pick it up in Miami. I have the rest of the files in my room."

He grabbed her hand and dragged her inside the house. "I want to see the papers. Now."

She wrestled out of his tight grip. "Gladly, but stop acting like a caveman. No need to kill the messenger," she said stalking ahead of him, her head high and her back stiff with indignation. She needed to cool her temper or they'd be at each other's throats and all because of his evil, greedy ex-wife.

He whirled her around and kissed her hard. "I'm mad at myself, not you. You're the best thing that's ever happened to me."

She kissed him back just as hard. "Good! That's how I feel about you."

"And that's why you're off the investigation as of this minute," he said, his mouth set in uncompromising lines.

Did he actually think she'd let him take over when there was so much at stake? "No way! This case is too important to me—to us.

I'm going to be right beside you all the way. I have the information you need, the contacts, the—"

"Forget it. Whether that gunshot in Miami was random or not, the killing of your cat wasn't," he said bluntly.

Her chest hitched. "I know and that's another reason why I'm not backing out. I need to avenge Slinky's death."

"And get killed in the process? I am not going to risk losing you," he said, his tone resolute.

She crossed her arms and thrust her chin high. "If you refuse to cooperate, I'm not giving you all the information."

"You play dirty." Nick's eyes narrowed into dangerous slits.

"I have to. I'm a reporter," she said smugly. "And besides, I love you. I'm not about to back down out of fear, not when we're this close to breaking the case wide open. You need me."

"I need you alive."

"Exactly, but if you won't work with me, I'll do it alone. I started this investig—"

"Damn it. Why do you have to be so pigheaded?" he bellowed, rubbing a hand over his face.

"I'm not being pigheaded. I know what I'm doing, Nick!"

"I know you do, Ronnie. But you're a target now. Aren't you the least bit afraid?"

"No," she said emphatically. "If I let fear get in the way of my work, I'll never get anything done."

"Aren't you afraid of anything?"

"Yes, but not physical danger. I'm afraid of the emotional stuff," she said, wishing he hadn't asked it.

He studied her with curious eyes. "What do you mean?"

"Nevermind. This isn't the time to get into it." She couldn't tell him her biggest fear was that he'd change his mind about wanting her. "I am not backing down on this case, Nick. Work with me or you get nothing."

Nick swore under his breath. He looked up at the ceiling, dragged in a deep breath and expelled it forcefully. When his blazing eyes met her eyes, his face and neck were crimson. "I don't like your tactics. We're wasting valuable time arguing."

"So quit arguing already." She stood before him, square-shouldered and inflexible, with a determined gleam in her eyes.

His jaw clamped tight and the skin on his face tightened as he grasped her shoulders and hauled her upward until his steely eyes bored into hers. Standing before him on tiptoe, she raised her chin and stared him down.

"You think you're invincible, Ronnie, but you're not," he said, shaking his head. "You're good at what you do, but I refuse to be the source of your danger. If I agree, you have to follow my lead to stay safe. Agreed?"

She stared at him, speechless with exasperation. He was acting like she was an amateur and all because he wanted to protect her. She was damn good at her job, had always managed to stay out of harm's way.

His fingers tightened on her shoulders. "Agreed?" he urged.

"Agreed," she said, backing down only because she'd already pushed him to the limit.

"I'll hold your feet to the fire," he warned, releasing her shoulders.

"Fine. But just remember we're partners."

While he didn't agree to the "partners" part, he didn't disagree either. She took that as a good sign.

"We'll leave for Miami first thing tomorrow morning," Nick said.

"Okay. I'll make the travel arrangements."

"Good. Now show me those papers. Don't wait up for me. I'll probably stay up all night reading them," he said evenly.

CHAPTER 19

hile Nick retreated to his office with the files, Veronique called her childhood campmate and hotel heiress, Theodora Behr.

"Hey, Teddy. It's Ronnie," Veronique said, missing her Heart Sister the minute she heard her cheery greeting.

"Ronnie!" Teddy squealed. "It's about time you called! Where the hell have you been?"

"I'm on the Gulf Coast of Florida, and I just survived Hurricane Abby."

"Ha, I'll bet. Nothing ever changes. Where there's a story, Veronique Whitcomb is on the scene. When do I get to see you?"

"Actually... I was calling because I need a favor."

"Okay, what's up?"

"I'm heading to Miami with a friend."

"A friend? Male or female?" Teddy asked with a chuckle in her voice.

"Male, but I can't get into it," Veronique said quickly before Teddy wanted details. There was nothing she enjoyed more than discussing romance.

"Aw, why not?"

"Because it's complicated."

"When isn't it complicated?" Teddy teased.

"I know, right? Anyway, I was wondering if you can get us a room at The Riviera for tomorrow night. I tried booking one, but there are no vacancies." The Riviera Hotel was Teddy's family's luxury oceanfront hotel in South Beach, Miami.

"Hmm, could be because they've just started a massive renovation. I'll call Sylvia now and make sure she works her magic to get you a room." Sylvia was Teddy's father's executive secretary and Teddy's surrogate mother since she'd lost her mom at a young age. "In whose name should I make the reservation?" she drawled playfully.

"Mine," Veronique said, wishing she could say, "Make it in Nick Cameron's name" instead. Teddy would've jumped up and down for joy and then gleefully tormented and teased her.

"Okay."

"Thanks a million. Where are you living now?" Veronique asked.

"I'm in Paris for the fall. After that, who knows?"

"Oops, sorry for calling so late. It must be way after midnight there."

"It is, but no worries. You know I'm nocturnal."

"Are you coming to Miami anytime soon?"

"Probably not. I have a few trips planned around some weddings I'm invited to."

No surprise there. Teddy was the quintessential "it" girl, traipsing through the world, learning new languages and making friends everywhere she went. It would take a lot to make her frisky feet touch land one day. Without knowing her as well as Veronique and Natasha did, anyone would think she was shallow, but there wasn't a shallow bone in her body. Teddy had a heart of gold and was generous to a fault, but her penchant for partying hard often landed her in trouble.

"Let's plan a reunion over Christmas. I've missed you and

Tash," Veronique said. They always made it a point to meet at least once a year.

"Yes, let's!" Teddy cried enthusiastically. "Anywhere you want to meet up. You know I avoid going home since *the amoeba* put a hex on my father," she said in a droll voice. "The amoeba" was Lola, Teddy's young bombshell stepmother, who'd swooped in and married Teddy's father when he was grieving over his wife's death. "We could go skiing and stay at Daddy's Swiss chalet or go someplace warm like St. Bart's."

"Sounds like a plan. I'll see what Natasha wants to do and get back to you," Veronique said, even though she hoped she'd be spending Christmas with Nick. Maybe the girls could come to Starfish Island instead...

Stop being a dreamer, she thought, mentally slapping herself. It was going to take a lot of perseverance and trust to get there, but she wouldn't go down without trying.

"Sweet!" Teddy blew noisy kisses into the phone. "Talk to you soon, Ronnie. Can't wait for our Heart Sister reunion."

"Me too. Bye, Teddy," Veronique said, grinning at Teddy's smooches. With keen anticipation of their trip to Miami, she opened her suitcase and began to pack.

NICK'S HANDS formed white-knuckled fists as he stood stock-still before his desk. His head pounded and his gut roiled as he read the files containing evidence of Elizabeth's fraudulent activities. As everything became clearer, his body shook with rage at his ex-wife and her lover's treachery, but mostly he was livid with himself. He'd been a damn fool all these months, retreating from humanity to lick his wounds when he should have been at the forefront protecting his foundation from piranhas like Elizabeth and Zack. There was no doubt in his mind they were smugly syphoning the charity funds to Macau, and planning to laugh all the way to the bank when Zack got out of jail.

He should have done what Ronnie had done, investigated Elizabeth's activities, going down to the schools and checking on them himself. He'd been too busy reeling from his own pain, feeling sorry for himself, to act on anything else. *Stupid. Stupid. Stupid.* He felt like kicking himself ten times over for being so blind and self-centered. If Ronnie hadn't gone with her sixth sense and investigated Elizabeth, it might have been too late to save his foundation. He owed her big time. He would never call her a snoop again or tease her about being so inquisitive. Her inquisitiveness had saved his ass.

He poured himself a two finger shot of Scotch. Taking a satisfying pull of the amber liquid, he began to formulate a plan on what he needed to do. As soon as they got the crucial piece of evidence in Miami, he'd call his lawyer, Fred Golden, and give him instructions. He'd have Fred meet with each board member individually, present the evidence and suggest a motion to dismiss Elizabeth as CEO. If they balked, Fred would then threaten to go to the authorities, which could result in very damaging information and charges of fraud, money laundering and tax evasion. That would harm the foundation and scare the crap out of the trustees. In addition, they could potentially be charged with negligence of duties resulting in loss of resources to the foundation. By the time he finished with Elizabeth, she'd be dismissed as CEO and compelled to return every last dime to the foundation.

Then, he'd resume his rightful place as CEO.

Early the next morning, Nick stuffed the papers into their respective files and threw them in a briefcase along with several wads of cash and his passport. Adrenaline pumped through his veins with an overload of drive and pure grit for restitution.

AFTER A QUICK BREAKFAST, Veronique headed to her room while Nick packed his suitcase. She was running around the room, straightening it up and throwing things in her suitcase, when he came by later.

"Meet me upstairs when you're finished. I'll be in my office," he said.

His office? That was huge validation and cause for celebration. When he left, Veronique hugged herself ecstatically. Nick had just invited her into his private man cave. *He trusted her.* She'd been worried sick when he never came to bed last night, wondering if he was upset with her.

The door was open when she approached Nick's office. The room was a large rectangle, lined on three sides with floor-to-ceiling book shelves filled with an impressive collection of books. The fourth wall was all windows. A large, sleek mahogany desk and a coffee colored leather armchair stood front and center. The room smelled of leather and Scotch, masculine and virile just like Nick. She saw the open bottle of Scotch and the glass beside it on the sideboard. She glanced at the large leather recliner on the far side of the wall, next to one of the bookcases. He must have slept there last night.

Nick stood in front of a panoramic window, his legs braced apart, shoulders squared and hands in his pockets. In deep contemplation, he gazed out at the large expanse of Turquoise Bay.

"Wow, that's some view you have up here," she said, coming up behind him. She put her arms around his waist and leaned her cheek on his broad back.

He turned and looped his arm around her waist nestling her against his side. "The gulf is as still as glass today. Shame we have to leave," he murmured, staring out at the ocean.

Her eyes followed his gaze. Sun rays lit the calm sea, turning it shimmering shades of turquoise. The sky was a clear cerulean blue, with no clouds in sight. A flock of pelicans flew in sync in the horizon.

"It's so beautiful here. I'd much rather spend the day on the beach again," she said. "With you."

He tilted her chin and gave her a toe-curling kiss. "When we get back, we'll have time to linger at the beach."

Her heart leapt with joy. *He was planning on bringing her back!*

"Promise?" she whispered, her breath catching with excitement as a familiar, restless ache began to build inside her.

"Yeah." He kissed the tip of her nose and pulled away. "If we don't leave now, you're going to end up on that desk," he taunted with a sexy smile.

Seductive images of them making love on the smooth mahogany desk sent ripples of desire coursing through her. How would the smooth wood feel against her skin? Her legs nearly buckled as she watched Nick's confident, long-limbed stride when he ambled to the door. Powerful and so damned sexy, even in the way he walked, Nick made her mouth water and her palms grow damp.

"Wait!" she called out. "Is this your mom?" She stopped next to his desk and lifted a silver frame with the picture of a slim young woman beside a little boy, holding an infant girl in her arms.

"Yeah. She was about your age in that picture," he said, his blue eyes turning vulnerable.

"She's so beautiful. You look like her, Nick, with your blue eyes and dark hair." Veronique smiled warmly. "Except that you're twice her size."

"Do you have pictures of your sister?"

He took a framed picture from his bookshelf. "This is Angela, my little sis," he said, showing her a picture of a young woman with the same coloring, startling blue eyes and long dark hair.

"She's so pretty. How old is she?"

"Thirty-one. She's a middle school teacher in New York."

"My hat's off to her. That's a tough age to teach. Is she single?"

"Yes. No more questions now. We need to leave." He ushered her out of the room and locked his office door.

"We're all set with hotel reservations. I also have a flash drive of everything that's in the files," she said, descending the stairs with him.

He paused at the bottom of the stairs. "Good. Where are the originals? Not in your apartment, I hope."

She put her hands on her hips and tilted her head, her eyebrows crinkling over narrowed eyes. "Of course not. They're in a bank vault. I only brought the hard copies because I figured you might lose power and then I wouldn't be able to show you anything."

"Good thinking," he said, punctuating it with a sound kiss. He held her shoulders and gazed deeply into her eyes. "I'm very proud of you. And impressed. You're one hell of a reporter. Thanks for everything."

"You're more than welcome, darling," she drawled, smiling at him. "Too bad we couldn't have stayed in your office and finished what you suggested."

"There's always tonight," he said, sliding his hands down her waist and cupping her buttocks.

The feel of his solid desire pressed against her sent ripples of desire coursing through her flushed body and her knees nearly buckled.

Nick gave her another slow, thorough kiss that made her tingle to her toes, and then he released her with a lusty slap on her bottom. "Okay, partner. Let's go move mountains."

CHAPTER 20

*V*eronique couldn't believe how quickly and efficiently everything went the remainder of the afternoon. They arrived in Miami by noon and then sped over to Maya's brother's loft apartment in the downtown area near the American Airlines Arena. Nick stayed in the car while Veronique went upstairs to meet with Maya. As promised, she texted him the minute she left the apartment so he knew she was safe. She wasn't used to working with a partner and it was hard accepting Nick's insistence on her safety above all else. For now she'd go along with his precautions.

"How did it go?" Nick asked when she got in the car.

"It went well. Maya gave me the document signed by Elizabeth and she filled me in on what she was dealing with at the office. She's very pretty and nice. Unfortunately, her boss sexually harassed her from the moment she started working there. When she complained, nobody took her seriously. No wonder she left."

Nick shook his head. "Can't blame her. Was her brother there?"

"No, she was alone. When she contacted me about the document, I told her not to tell *anyone* about it."

"Good. I hope she listened to you."

"She told me nobody knows besides us, not even her brother or her fiancé. She was pretty relieved to hand over the document."

"I'll bet."

Veronique sighed. "I told her about Slinky's death and she was horrified. She said she wouldn't be surprised if Elizabeth was behind it and called her ruthless."

"She is, but she'll be stopped soon enough," Nick said and stepped on the pedal. He squeezed Veronique's hand. "Good job, partner."

"Thanks," Veronique said, relishing the solid feel of his hand engulfing hers.

They coasted down Biscayne Bay and onto the MacArthur Causeway, enjoying the sites of enormous, luxury cruise ships lined up on the water. When they got to Miami Beach, Ocean Drive was a pastel prism of art deco design. They rolled down the windows and watched a crowd of tourists, students and hipsters milling down the sidewalk, eating in the cafes and dancing in the nightclubs. The party spilled onto the sidewalk as the ethnically diverse crowd pulsed to a tropical beat that was inviting and infectious.

Before going to the hotel, they went to Shake Shack for take-out cheeseburgers and fries and ate them in the car. By the time Nick pulled into the circular entrance of The Riviera Hotel, it was getting dark and a smattering of stars began to appear in the sky. They stepped out of the car and waited for the valet to unload their suitcases. The night air was warm and sultry, fragrant with flowering jasmine and the Atlantic Ocean breeze.

"Wait till you see this hotel in the daylight," Veronique said. "It's gorgeous and majestic without being excessive. I was surprised when Teddy told me they're starting a massive renovation."

"Why were you surprised?" Nick asked.

"Because the hotel isn't that old. It must be her stepmother who's pushing it. Teddy can't stand her."

He slanted a meaningful look at her. "Evil stepmother?"

"Yeah, definitely."

"Will Teddy be here?"

"No, I wish. She and Tash would adore seeing you again."

"It'd be nice to see them too. What are they doing these days?"

"Natasha is in previews for a new musical on Broadway, and Teddy's living the life in Paris. She's The Riviera's social ambassador," Veronique said, grinning.

Nick gave a dry chuckle. "That doesn't surprise me."

THE HOTEL SUITE was sumptuous and more than Veronique had expected when she'd asked Teddy for a room. It was so like generous Teddy to make sure they got a fabulous one. Nick tipped the bellman and strolled out to the balcony while Veronique freshened up in the bathroom.

Glancing at the imported bath gels and body lotion on the sleek white marble counter, she couldn't wait to take a hot bath. She splashed her face with cool water, brushed her teeth and ran her fingers through her hair. The layers had curled up due to the humidity, but she didn't care. After the power outage from Hurricane Abby, she'd enjoyed the liberty of letting her curls go free and untamed. She smiled and hugged herself happily remembering how Nick had buried his face in her hair and told her he loved her sexy curls.

She exited the bathroom and toured the spacious adjoining areas. The living room/dining room was decorated in cool, muted tones of taupe and pale gray, from the designer furniture to the walls and drapes. A large basket filled with a pineapple, clementine tangerines, green grapes, strawberries and bananas awaited them next to a white bakery box filled with The Riviera's famous oversized assorted cookies. She opened the box and had a hard time deciding on which cookie to eat. They'd skipped dessert after dinner and she was in the mood for something sweet.

Veronique bit into a crisp chocolate chunk cookie studded with meaty walnuts and swooned. "Yum! These cookies are delicious. Want one?" she asked Nick.

"No, thanks. Come join me outside," he said.

"In a minute. I want to check out the badroom. Ha, I meant bedroom," she said with a giggle.

Nick gave a short bark of laughter. "Badroom sounds good to me."

"Me too." She was still smiling when she entered the bedroom. The king-size bed was decked out in luxurious bed linens and already turned down with chocolate truffles on a tiny silver tray on each pillow. She would have to thank Teddy and Sylvia first thing tomorrow morning for providing one of their finest suites, fit for a honeymoon.

"There's an oversize tub in the bathroom," she called out. "Big enough for two."

Nick appeared at the bedroom door straight away. He'd shaved that morning, but evening stubble on the sharp planes of his handsome face gave him a sexy edge. The collar of his pinstriped, button down shirt was open at the throat and untucked, the sleeves rolled up on his strong forearms. He leaned against the doorframe, gazing at her with a seductive smile and arresting midnight blue eyes.

"Ah, so you'd rather have me than a cookie," she teased, her pulse tripping up.

He stepped out of his shoes and headed toward her. "You're the only sweet I plan on eating tonight." He unbuttoned his shirt and pulled off his pants, tossing them on the bed before he reached her. "Get out of those clothes, baby, or I'll strip you down myself," he growled.

"Go ahead. I'm waiting…" she taunted, looking at him over her shoulder with a naughty smile. She turned and arched her back, her head tilted so she could see him while he unzipped her dress.

Nick's eyes caught on hers, burning with carnal intensity and the promise of fierce lovemaking. "You like to play with fire," he murmured into her ear, his breath warm and tickly as his hands slid down her sides, squeezing and caressing the indentation of her waist, the swell of her hips. She leaned her head back and closed her eyes with a breathless moan of anticipation. A tight, coiling surge of desire made her knees buckle as she slumped against him.

Nick's strong hands on her hips held her steady as his lips brushed the back of her neck and traveled down her spine. Inch by inch, he unzipped the dress and revealed her creamy skin, pressing kisses on her flushed skin along the way. With a practiced flick, he unsnapped her bra and slid his warm hands around her torso to cup her cool, bare breasts. His blunt fingertips tweaked her sensitive nipples, sending jolts of pleasure so acute her skin tingled and moist heat gathered between her thighs.

"I want you now," he whispered, his voice raw, his breath hot with desire in the sensitized shell of her ear.

"Yes," she breathed, caught up in a whirlwind of pleasurable sensations. He nipped the back of her neck and goose bumps spread over her skin as thrilling tingles made her moan huskily.

"I'm going to bury myself inside you. I want all of your tight, sweet warmth, over and over again," he murmured, his voice gravelly and hoarse.

He spun her around and held her face between his hands as he kissed her deeply, his tongue mimicking what his body would be doing to her soon. Her dress and bra slipped off and landed in a pile around her ankles. His thumbs hooked into her silk panties and slid them down her shaky legs to join her dress. She stepped forward, her breasts pebbling into hard pinpoints as they rubbed against his hard chest. She clung to him naked and vulnerable, *wanting, wanting, wanting*.

Sliding his arms under her thighs, his broad palms cupped her buttocks and hoisted her up. She wrapped her legs around his waist and gripped his shoulders. His thick arousal pressed against her as he backed her to the wall.

Veronique gasped when he entered her in one neat stroke. Naked and primed for urgent lovemaking, their bodies fused together. She was so wet and violently aroused, she could scarcely breathe as he surged inside her, each stroke stronger, deeper than the last. Her pelvis lurched forward, taking in the raw hunger of his passion. His slow, deliberate thrusts made her go wild. She threw her head back and moaned loudly, so close, so close, her body began to implode. She couldn't take another second. Pure, frenzied pleasure burst through her as she spiraled out of control, panting raggedly, writhing and crying out her release.

"That's right, baby, shout it out," he urged, his voice savage. "Open your eyes," he commanded and looked deep into her eyes. "You're mine. Mine," he grunted, punctuating each word with greedy thrusts culminating in a vigorous climax.

"Yes, Nick. Yours," she cried, quivering as delicious tremors of release rocked her senses.

Their bodies still joined, he walked her to the bed.

"Nick," she whispered when the thrilling aftershocks subsided and she lay beside him in a blissful daze.

"Hmm?" His voice was a low, sexy rumble in his chest.

She propped up on her forearms and looked into his sated, heavy-lidded eyes. "Did you mean it when you said we're going back when we're done with business here?" She smiled hesitantly and added, "I mean...am I going back with you?"

"Yes, baby. I'm not letting you out of my sight. I can't imagine home without you in it."

Struck speechless at the certainty in his tone, her heart soared. "Thank you," she said, when she found her voice.

"My pleasure…definitely mine," he murmured, turning her on her side and spooning her. He pressed a kiss on the side of her neck and nuzzled it.

"Let's take a hot, leisurely soak in that big tub," she said after a languorous pause.

"Rest now, bathe later," he said, smoothing her curls from her face as he wrapped a heavy arm around her waist and hugged her close.

"Okay," she agreed readily, exhilarated at the thought of going back to Starfish Island with Nick. She sighed dreamily and closed her eyes.

It didn't get any better than this.

CHAPTER 21

The next morning, Nick was all business. By seven he had showered, shaved and was dressed in a starched blue business shirt and tan tailored slacks that drew attention to his powerful physique and presence. Veronique's face lit up with a proud smile, watching him in action. He was in his element, commanding and forthright while he talked to Fred on the phone in the living room area.

Giving him privacy to discuss his affairs, she stepped away from the doorway and called room service. Ravenous after their incredible night together, she ordered a potato, mushroom and gruyere omelet with buttered toast for Nick and a Belgian waffle with strawberries for herself. Adding orange juice and champagne for mimosas and a pot of coffee, she hung up and got ready. After the luxurious, hot bath last night, she just needed to get dressed and run her fingers through her hair to give it shape.

Twenty minutes later, she heard a knock on the door and ran to answer it. "Room service is here," she crowed on her way to the door.

The server wheeled in a table covered with a white tablecloth. Two silver domed plates, a carafe of coffee, a bottle of champagne and a pitcher of fresh-squeezed orange juice were arranged around a small bouquet of spring flowers.

Nick tipped the server and when he left, he lifted each dome and looked inside. "Looks good. Glad you ordered champagne too."

Veronique couldn't contain her joyful smile. She was thrilled to her toes to be having breakfast in a gorgeous suite with the gorgeous man she loved.

"Will you pour us some mimosas?"

"Sure," Nick said, simultaneously pouring the champagne and orange juice into crystal flutes with two hands.

He handed her a glass, and she raised it to him. "To the CEO of The Cameron Hope Foundation," she toasted with a warm smile.

Nick clinked his glass with hers. "And to the best investigative reporter I know."

"Aw, thank you. How did your call go with Fred?"

"It went very well. He's calling the other board members to meet with each one individually."

"I just want everything to be resolved right away. I hate the waiting part."

"Me too, baby. Let's watch the news." He turned on the TV with the remote control and switched channels until he landed on a national news station.

They ate with the news in the background on low volume.

"Yum, this waffle is delicious. I wonder who the chef is now. Teddy knows all the celebrity chefs in South Beach and she was trying to get—"

"Fuck!" Nick suddenly shouted. He shot up from the table, knocking over his coffee and scaring the living daylights out of Veronique.

"What's wrong?" she asked, alarmed when she saw his livid face. She nervously blotted the spilled coffee with her cloth napkin as he raised the volume.

Nick didn't utter a word. His rapt attention was riveted to the screen.

Veronique followed his gaze and choked on the bit of waffle in her mouth when she saw Nick's picture on the screen with a banner across that said, "Breaking News."

Listening intently, Nick didn't move a muscle. His face was a shocked mask of disbelief as the veteran anchorwoman, Carla Kincaid, spoke.

"Reclusive billionaire Nick Cameron has been living on Starfish Island on the Gulf Coast for the past six months," Carla said. "We bring you ACE News reporter, Veronique Whitcomb's first hand report." She chuckled and shook her head. "And from the likes of it, the hunky corporate raider may soon become an instant heartthrob sensation."

The videotape opened with a sweeping panorama of his house and the land surrounding it, then it focused on Nick, bare-chested and chiseled in low rise jeans working in the yard. Close-ups of his face in deep concentration played on the screen as Veronique's voice narrated, "Hurricane Abby tore apart Nick's paradise, but that hasn't deterred him. He's powerful and unstoppable." At the end of the segment, the camera zoomed in on the picture of him she'd taken in his closet when he was covered in dusty plaster.

"Uh oh." Carla chuckled and turned to her co-anchor. "Looks like there's going to be trouble in paradise!"

"Oh no," Veronique mumbled, her hand going to her mouth. She closed her eyes tightly. She couldn't bear to look—it was unbelievable, strange…and disturbing. Her camera had been in her suitcase the whole time, underneath her clothes. No one had been inside the house but her and Nick. How had this happened? Her stomach constricted into a knot of anguish and her throat went dry. She could barely form words, terrified to meet Nick's eyes.

"I'm just as stunned as you are," she said, her voice strangled.

"*You're* stunned." He faced her, his eyes blazing with cynicism, the corners of his mouth turned down harshly.

"Yes. I have no idea how that video was leaked. I never meant anyone to see it but me. And especially not you!" she cried, her whole world crashing down.

"Who *are* you?" he demanded, his tone razor-sharp with censure.

"I'm Ronnie, the girl who loves you," she said, her heart squeezing painfully. She grabbed his arm. "Don't look at me that way, Nick. It's true. I told you I've loved you since I was a little girl." She felt awkward saying it, like she was begging him to love her back, but she had to. Earlier this week, he'd finally told her he trusted her. She couldn't let that trust be destroyed by an inexplicable turn of events.

He shook her off and turned away. His body rigid, he stalked to the bedroom.

"Nick! Please. Listen to me," she pleaded.

Ignoring her calls, he threw his belongings into his suitcase and snapped it shut.

She raced to his side, her heart thudding at harrowing speed as she tried to breathe. She grappled with shallow breaths, gulping air into her tight chest, trying not to hyperventilate.

She grabbed her purse and pulled out her camera. "Look my camera's in my purse. It's never been out of my possession!"

His eyes, sharp blue glass shards, sliced through her heart with accusation. "You fed it to the press to boost your career. What's next, the inside scoop?"

"Stop it! How can you say such a despicable thing?" she asked, devastated he could think so little of her. "Is that what you believe? That I'm a selfish person who'd sell your soul for my gain?"

"Spare me your lies," he said furiously.

Scalding indignation rose inside of her, scorching every pore of her body. "I'm *innocent*, Nick!"

"You lied when you said you wouldn't take any more pictures. I should have known not to trust you," he said scathingly.

She flinched at his brutal tone. Thick, bitter humiliation clogged her throat as she blinked back burning tears. She bit her lower lip to stop it from trembling, but her chin quivered pitifully.

Don't cry, don't cry, don't cry.

She put her hands out in supplication, hoping to reach the Nick she'd been intimate with all week...the Nick she loved. "Nick, please be reasonable. Don't you remember what it feels like to be falsely accused?"

His jaw unyielding, his mouth formed a grim line as his eyes turned chillingly somber. "I do remember. Very clearly in fact. I've already dealt with one treacherous woman. I won't deal with another," he said, his face frozen, his eyes uncompromising. "I'm done."

His words tore into her like a thousand daggers, shredding the last of her hope.

"You can't mean that," she pleaded, but her pleas landed on deaf ears as he stalked away.

"Nick!" she shouted and fell to her knees. Tremors of despair racked her body, rendering her helpless to rise from the floor.

He walked out and slammed the door behind him.

Hugging her quaking body, Veronique told herself it was a nightmare and that she'd wake up soon. But it was real and too convoluted for her to figure out.

She lay huddled on the ground for a long time, unable to get up, unable to even cry, shell-shocked beyond tears and words. Why? How had this happened? They'd been alone in the house the whole time. She'd fallen so deeply in love with Nick, she couldn't imagine him disposing of her that way. As if she meant nothing to him.

The scene played itself in her mind over and over again, not making any sense and making her feel more panicked by the moment.

I've already dealt with one treacherous woman. I won't deal with another. I'm done. Nick's callous words broke her heart with their awful finality. The look of bitter condemnation in his eyes would remain imprinted in her mind forever.

Veronique covered her face and toppled over sideways as sobs rose from her chest and tore through her throat. Her tears let loose and poured out of her eyes like a waterfall. She sobbed until she was limp with exhaustion.

Nick was gone.

CHAPTER 22

*N*ick tipped the valet, threw his suitcase in the car's trunk and slammed it shut. When he got in the car and turned on the ignition, his sunglasses fogged up from the steam heat trapped inside. Even after being parked in the hotel garage, the interior was hot enough to cook a meal, but it was nothing compared to how steamed he was. His hands shook as he cranked up the air conditioner and aimed the vents at his face, welcoming the cold blast of air on his fevered skin.

More than anything, I want to restore my reputation as a first class journalist.

Ronnie had said it a few days ago when he'd asked her what she wanted most in life. He should have processed that with his mind instead of letting his lust take over. She was no longer the pesky tomboy who'd bedeviled him years ago with her antics. She had become an enticing temptress, and he'd been powerless to resist her from the minute she'd come traipsing into his house. All smiles and banter and sparkling emerald eyes, she'd teased and tormented him until he'd given in and taken his pleasure with her fiercely on the beach.

Her sweet surrender had been his undoing.

Once he'd gotten a taste of burying himself in her tight, velvety sheath, he hadn't been the same. She was a sweet, sultry addiction, tormenting him with her honeyed taste, the silkiness of her skin, the lushness of her pert curves. He was insatiable when it came to Ronnie, an animal ensnared by her scent, needing to satiate his cravings as often as he could and even that wasn't enough. As soon as he was done pleasuring her and wringing out the last drop, he would begin to want her again. Hell, he was hard now just thinking about it.

She had sunk her seductive claws in him deep enough to scar. How could she have pretended to be someone so sincere and caring? He hadn't seen Ronnie in fifteen years, and against his better judgment, he'd allowed her to stay, to get under his skin and work her spell on him, robbing him of rational thought. All this time, she'd had a deceitful plan to get a prized story on him. The proof was in the tape she'd made.

He was a hot mess, but he couldn't let his dark fury cloud his judgment, especially when Ronnie was in danger because of him.

Cursing loudly, he got out of the car and headed back to the room.

VERONIQUE RAISED her head from the living room floor when she heard the door open. Through a thick veil of tears and damp hair, she watched Nick storm into the room.

She sat up and cried out joyfully, "Nick! You came back!"

"Get up," he said briskly, pulling her up beside him. "You're coming with me."

She smoothed her hair back from her tear streaked face and wiped her eyes. "I couldn't imagine you would be so mean and untrusting. I'm glad you came to your senses," she said, wondering at his tight grip on her wrist and the merciless glint in his eyes.

"Not quite. If your life wasn't at stake, I'd leave you here," he said, his mouth twisting.

His words felt like a sharp slap across the face. "Really? Then leave," she retorted, fuming at his nerve. Thrusting her chin high, she crossed her arms over her chest and glared at him. "I'm not going with you until you tell me you don't believe that I sold you out."

"You don't have a choice," he said darkly, grabbing her arm.

"Yes, I do," she said shaking him off. "I'm not some damsel in distress who needs rescuing!"

"You're coming with me because you're not safe here. Plus, I need the information you have in New York for tomorrow's meeting." Nick's jaw ticked dangerously as he opened her suitcase. "Quit arguing and pack your things. Or I will!"

THE NEXT SIX hours were the longest and most tedious Veronique had ever spent as they drove to the airport, boarded a plane to LaGuardia and hailed a taxi when they got there.

When she heard Nick give the taxi driver Fred and Maman's address on the Upper West Side, she leaned forward and told the cabbie, "Please take me to midtown west first. It's on the corner of Broadway and—"

He turned to Nick with questioning eyes. "Where do I go first?"

"Don't listen to her. We're going to 74th and Central Park West," Nick told the driver firmly. He turned to Veronique. "You can't get off first. I have a crucial meeting with Fred before he meets with the board tomorrow. Visit with your mother while I'm there."

The nerve of Nick acting like a despot in front of the cab driver and telling her what to do! Not that she cared what the driver thought. He'd already shown himself to be sexist by ignoring her request.

She tapped on the driver's shoulder. "Drop him off first and then take me to Broadway and—"

"No, lady. I'm going where your husband told me to go," he replied with infuriating chauvinism. "You two can fight it out there."

"Well!" Veronique huffed and flounced to the far side of the car. "For the record, he's not my husband," she said with disdain.

"Damn right I'm not," Nick said rudely.

It wasn't the time or place for arguing, but Veronique wished she could tell him off for treating her like a traitor. He had accused her and convicted her of betraying him without even giving her a chance to figure out what had happened. She looked out of the window in stony silence, acutely aware of Nick's tightly restrained fury as he sat on the other side checking his email. When the taxi finally arrived at Fred's apartment, Nick gave him a generous tip and nudged Veronique toward the building where Willie, the elderly doorman who was an institution there, stood at the entrance.

"Hello, Mr. Cameron. It's been a long time since I've seen you round here," Willie said, smiling broadly. He nodded at Veronique. "Same for you, missy. Do you two know each other?" he asked, glancing at their suitcases.

"Yes, unfortunately," Veronique said through tight lips. "Nice to see you, Willie. Would you keep my suitcase here until I come down?"

"Mine too," Nick said, rolling his suitcase forward.

"Sure thing. Have a great day, all," Willie said, beaming.

"Thanks," Nick said, giving him a tip. He placed his hand on the small of Veronique's back and ushered her to the elevator.

Veronique moved away as if his touch scalded her. "Don't touch me," she hissed.

He dropped his hand and entered the elevator after her. Nick's hardnosed, dominant presence beside her made her want to scream. He was making her wait at her mother's apartment while he took care of business. It wasn't fair. She had uncovered the case, done all the legwork and now he was making her play it safe while he got to enjoy all the action. She wanted the satisfaction of seeing Elizabeth stopped and reprehended.

The overwhelmingly sad taste of loneliness and rejection made her realize she should make the best of this visit with Maman. It was long overdue. She was tired of being estranged from her mother and tired of blaming her for a lot of her childhood angst.

Nick rapped sharply on the door, startling her from her musings. His face was cold and unreadable, and she could feel his barely restrained contempt for her. It felt so awful to be on the receiving end of his anger that she moaned out loud before she could stop herself.

He turned to her with a chilling look, one she'd never forget, and then the door opened. She blinked at Maman and was heartened when her mother's green eyes lit up with wonder.

"Nick! Veronique! What brings the two of you together?" Helene asked with a surprised smile.

"Hello, Miss Helene, I've brought your errant daughter," Nick said, kissing Helene's cheek.

"I'm so happy you did." Helene beamed at Nick, and then held out her arms to Veronique. "I've missed you so much, *ma 'tite cherie*. Come, give me a hug." Her slender arms enveloped Veronique, smelling of tuberose and gardenia, scents that transported her back to her childhood. Maman's arms held her firmly, so different from long ago when she would barely give her a brief pat on the head before sending her off to bed with her nanny. Her affectionate greeting was a welcome surprise. She hadn't seen Maman since Christmas when Veronique had left after a dumb argument. So dumb, she couldn't even remember what they'd argued about.

"Thanks. I've missed you too," Veronique said. "I don't know why I let so much time go by without seeing you." Truth was, she had avoided seeing her and Fred because she hadn't wanted to deal with their cross-examination over her demotion at work.

"I have to leave. I'll let you two get caught up," Nick said, patting Helene's shoulder.

Helene released Veronique and gave him a quizzical look. "Where are you going?"

"I'm meeting Fred at his office. I should be back in an hour. Don't let Veronique out of your sight," he said, walking down the hall. "Keep her here till I get back."

Helene's eyebrows shot up at his gruff order. "Why?" she called after him.

"She's dangerous," he said in a flat tone and left.

"Dangerous? *You?* Why did he say that?" Helene asked Veronique when he was out of earshot. Her arched brows knitted over incredulous eyes as she closed the door. "What did he mean?"

Veronique rolled her eyes. "I don't know. Don't pay attention to him. Nick has a convoluted sense of humor," she said, brushing it off so she wouldn't harp on it. Nick thought she was untrustworthy and now he was calling her dangerous. It cut her to the quick, and also made her furious. Forcing herself to smile, she concentrated on her mother, not Nick, otherwise she'd scowl.

"Come sit beside me," Helene said, walking toward the sofa.

Veronique perched on the edge of the Victorian sofa, feeling as fragile as the antique mahogany legs. "Did you watch the news today?" she asked, amazed that Maman had no idea what Nick was talking about. She was thankful that Fred hadn't said a word to Helene about it. He was probably waiting to tell her tonight.

"Not yet. I was at the doctor's office for my yearly checkup and it took most of the afternoon. Has something happened?" Helene asked, looking worried.

"No. I was just wondering."

Helene leaned back and studied Veronique. "Where have you

been all this time? In the tropics? You skin is so tanned and your hair is..well, it's…" Her voice faltered as she grappled for words.

"Wild? Out of control?" Veronique prompted, self-consciously raking her fingers through her hair. She wouldn't let her mother make her feel gauche, not today when she had more important things to contend with than how polished she looked. "I like it this way," she said edgily. "Please don't criticize me. Can't we have a moment together without you judging what I'm wearing or how my hair looks?"

"I wasn't doing that. I was just making an observation, *cherie*. That's all," Helene said mildly. She patted Veronique's knee and smiled at her. "You look lovely and contrary to what you think, I'm very proud of you."

"You are?" Veronique couldn't hide her shock.

"Yes, you are a strong and fearless young woman—something I never was. In many ways you remind me of your Daddy. He had the same warm charisma that drew people."

Maman's kind words and sincere tone were a balm to her tattered feelings. "Thank you, that means the world to me. You know how much I adored Daddy."

Helene nodded. "You and me both, *cherie*."

She laid her soft hand on Veronique's cheek and gazed into her eyes with curiosity. "Tell me…how did you and Nick come here together?"

Veronique drew in a calming breath. The mere mention of Nick upset her and the more she thought of it, the more incensed she became. How dare he treat her that way? "It's a long story, and I'd rather not get into it."

"Fine. We won't talk about Nick, although…" Helene hesitated.

"Although what?" Veronique said uneasily. Did Maman know what had transpired between her and Nick? She couldn't imagine Nick telling Fred intimate details of his private life.

"I was going to say, 'although Fred and I think the world of him.' We never believed he was guilty."

"Neither did I. How are you feeling, Maman? You look great," Veronique said, quickly changing the subject.

It was true; Maman looked different than she had over the holidays. More centered. She still had a smooth auburn bob and porcelain skin with very few wrinkles for a fifty-year-old woman, but her green, catlike eyes had softened with age. In her royal blue, sleeveless dress and muted gold Tory Burch ballerina flats, she looked elegant and casual at once.

"Have you been doing anything different?" Veronique asked.

"I've taken up yoga and it's really helped with my mood swings," Helene said. "At my age, my hormones are all over the place."

"Oh." It couldn't only be the yoga; she seemed more at peace than ever. "How's Fred?"

"He's doing very well. Soon as he wraps up the case he's working on, we're going to Italy for a month."

"That should be fun. Fred makes you happy, doesn't he?"

Helene smiled. "Oh, yes. I don't know what I would have done without him all these years. He's my rock."

"You're lucky to have him. I admit I resented him for taking you away from me, but I realize now he's a good man. I'm sorry I gave you so much grief growing up," she said with an apologetic smile.

"It wasn't entirely your fault. You rebelled because I wasn't the best mother," Helene said, looking down at her hands. "I was so wrapped up in coping with your Daddy's problem, I left the child-raising to nannies and later to boarding school. Do you forgive me?" Her earnest eyes searched Veronique's.

"I already have, Maman," Veronique said, squeezing her hand gently. She wanted, *needed,* to make peace with her. She was done with past resentments. After Nick's parting comment and experiencing that level of heart wrenching pain and loss, she could empathize with her mother. "I understand now. All these years I blamed you for enabling Daddy, but it wasn't your fault. Daddy was a wonderful man, but he had a terrible addiction problem. I realize now that you loved him so much you couldn't bear to leave him. That's why you stood by him all those years."

"I see you understand. Thank you, *cherie*." Helene's eyes welled up with tears and her voice quivered as she asked, "What brought this on?"

Veronique gave a self-deprecating shrug. "I guess I grew up. I'm through judging others when I have room to talk." *If Maman only knew the depth of her love for Nick and the depth of her despair over losing him.*

"May I have another hug? One wasn't enough," Helene said, opening her arms.

"Of course." Veronique hugged her tightly and kissed her cheek. A warm feeling of closure settled over her as she rose from the sofa. "I have to go now."

Helene's face fell. "So soon? You just got here. Won't you stay for tea? With shortbread cookies?"

Veronique smiled. "Nothing has changed. You've been having Earl Grey tea with cookies since I was a little girl."

Helene chuckled. "And what's wrong with that?"

"Nothing. Nothing at all, but I can't stay longer. I'll come by next week to see you again."

"Promise?"

"Promise," Veronique said, meaning it.

"What will I tell Nick? He looked very stern when he told me not to let you out of my sight," Helene fretted.

"Tell him I went home," she said carelessly.

Helene looked doubtful. "I hope he doesn't get angry. I've never seen him look so tense."

"He'll get over it," Veronique said.

But *she* wouldn't. She would never get over the heartbreak he'd caused her.

CHAPTER 23

*D*aisy leaned back in Nick's office chair and put her feet on his desk, a smug smile curling her lips as she fingered the wads of cash she'd found stashed in the top drawer. *Pocket change*, she thought smirking. She wouldn't have to steal petty cash anymore. She was going to be very rich soon.

Finding Veronique's files had been a Godsend! She'd already made a nice bundle selling her video and the silly picture of Nick. She'd reached out to all the media channels and gotten the highest bid for them. Then she'd turned her efforts to extorting Nick's ex-wife, Elizabeth. When Elizabeth had balked, Daisy, pretending to be Veronique, had said, "I have stuff on your involvement with Nick's foundation and it doesn't make you look good. Know what I mean?"

Daisy had filled her in on the fat file of evidence and the ex-wife had wasted no time in arranging for a nice bundle of cash to be delivered to her near Nick's house. She glanced at her watch. Six-thirty. In half an hour, she would meet Hector, Elizabeth's "delivery man" at the corner of Begonia Way. She slid her hands over Nick's desk wondering if he had allowed Veronique into his private quarters. *Probably.* And they'd probably done it on his desk too. She felt sick. She should have been the one having sex with Nick, not that stupid bitch. She couldn't wait to bring her down. If Daisy couldn't have Nick, Veronique wouldn't have him either.

She wouldn't let it upset her; there were better things to think about. Daisy's newfound riches were intoxicatingly sweet—and so was her revenge. She got up and left the office, closing the door behind her. She had picked the lock earlier, laughing at how easy it had been and wishing she'd done it much sooner.

Intimately familiar with the order of things in Nick's master bedroom and closet, she gave it a sweeping glance and then went straight to his king size bed. She pulled the *Santería* medal out of her pocket and stared at it, willing it to work. The medal of Chango, the *Santería* god of thunder who dominated and over-came enemies, was just what she needed to rid herself—and Nick —of the bitch. She slid the medal across the top of Nick's bed from one edge to the other as she prayed fervently, "Chango, keep Veronique away from Nick. Get rid of her forever. Forev-er!" She kissed the medal and placed it under his mattress, feeling a surge of empowerment so strong, she shivered with excitement.

She ran to the guest room and opened all the drawers of the nightstand and dresser to see if Veronique had left anything behind. Good, they were empty. Maybe she didn't need Chango's help after all...maybe the bitch wasn't coming back. With a stab of disappointment, she remembered Veronique hadn't unpacked her suitcase while there. Of course the drawers would be empty. Her clothes had never been in them. The messy bitch had kept her stuff in a jumble and not even bothered to hang them up.

Daisy noticed the straw hat that Veronique had been wearing when she and Nick returned from the beach on the vanity counter. She stood in front of the mirror and twisted her long hair into a bun at the back of her head. She put the hat on and decided to keep it. It would be good for hiding her face when she met up with Elizabeth's delivery guy. Putting on her dark sunglasses, she exited the house through the back door.

As she rounded the corner, she made her way toward the driveway, kicking at rocks along the way. She glanced at the afternoon sun, glad there wasn't any rain to mar her perfect plan. She couldn't wait to get her hands on her stash. Five more minutes and she'd be at the designated spot for the drop off. She was caught up in making plans with the millions she'd soon have when her foot caught on an exposed Banyan root and she tripped.

A sudden, piercing pain ripped into the tip of her left shoulder. It felt as if someone had pressed a lit torch to her skin. She glanced at her shoulder and screamed when she saw the gaping hole.

She'd been shot!

She gripped her shoulder as searing pain flooded her shoulder and blood spurted on her hand. Collapsing to the ground, she landed facedown, her mouth grappling with grass and leaves as she tried to call for help. The smell of her blood seeping in the dirt increased her panicked terror. Groaning in pain, she struggled to rise on her elbows, but she couldn't summon enough strength as darkness closed over her.

CHAPTER 24

*N*ick and Fred walked back to Fred's apartment after their meeting as the sun set over the bustling city.

"I'm taking Helene to Marea tonight for dinner," Fred said. "Care to join us?"

Nick checked his wristwatch. "No thanks. It's already eight o'clock. Does Helene know about Ronnie's video?"

"I doubt it. She was out all day at the doctor's office. She said she was planning on taking a nap when she got home."

"We must have interrupted her nap," Nick said ruefully. "Well, she probably knows about it now. It's all over the news."

"That's inevitable. You've been an enigma to the press for the past six months. Everyone's been clamoring for your story."

"Nobody's getting it, not even your stepdaughter," Nick said roughly. "If it wasn't for the danger she's in, I'd never see Ronnie again, but I'm going to pick her up and take her to my place for safekeeping until we contact the authorities about Elizabeth's fraud."

"That won't be until after tomorrow's meeting," Fred said.

"I know."

Fred ran his fingers through his coarse, short cropped salt and pepper hair. "Look, I know you're angry, but try to be rational. I've known Ronnie since she was a kid. She might be impulsive and impossible to tame, but she's not a self-serving person. Far from it."

"Not impossible to tame." Nick had tamed her into a soft, purring kitten in his arms. The memory of it, and her subsequent treachery, only added to his ire. "Just impossible to trust," he said, the bitter taste of betrayal choking him.

Fred studied him with shrewd eyes. "You're not thinking logically. If Ronnie had done it to further her career, she would have written a story. She's a damn good journalist. Why would she deliver the tape like a lowly tabloid reporter?"

"We were the only ones in the house the whole week she was there," Nick said through tight lips.

"Still…" Fred said, shaking his head. "A lot of weird things have been happening lately. Maybe someone broke into your house and stole her camera."

"Nobody stole it. Her camera is in her purse. She said it was in her suitcase the whole time."

"Give her the benefit of the doubt," Fred said, clapping Nick on the shoulder. "And don't give up on her. She's one in a million."

"Whatever she did, I still intend on keeping her safe," Nick muttered.

The moment they arrived at Fred's apartment, Helene answered the door with a worried look.

"Where's Ronnie?" Nick asked.

"She went home soon after you left. I couldn't make her stay," Helene said with an exasperated sigh. "You know how headstrong she is."

"Unfortunately I do. I need to get going," Nick said hurriedly. He kissed Helene's cheek and raised a hand in farewell to Fred, exchanging a meaningful look with him.

. . .

WHEN HE LEFT, Nick hailed a taxi straight away to Ronnie's studio apartment. Every time he tried calling her it went to voice mail. Damn her! It was just like Ronnie to do what she wanted, when she wanted to. He cursed under his breath, a string of curses so vile, the taxi driver chuckled.

He bounded up the three flights of stairs to her studio apartment, two at a time. When he got to her door, he knocked on it repeatedly and called out, "Ronnie! Open the door." He was out of patience and she was purposely making him wait outside, ignoring him like a stranger.

"You looking for Veronique?" A lanky, rumpled-looking teenager scratched his belly below his torn T shirt and eyed Nick with interest.

"Yes. Do you know her?" Nick said curtly.

He yawned and rubbed his eyes. It was a little early for a teen to be sleepy. He was probably stoned. "Sure, man. She just left."

"Did she say where she was going?"

"Nope, but she ran down the stairs like she was on fire."

"Thanks," Nick said and ran down like he was on fire too.

When he reached the bottom step, he checked the tracker on his phone and found Ronnie was in the Upper West Side. Thank God, he'd had the foresight to synchronize their phones so he could keep track of her. When he arrived at the destination, he stood outside the building and called her, but it went to voice mail.

"Damn it, quit playing games! I'm downstairs and I need to talk to you," he said, leaving a terse message. *Again.*

VERONIQUE SAT in Natasha's apartment with her heart in her throat. She loved going to Natasha's place and being in a Broadway performer's digs. It was beautifully decorated in soft cream and apricot colors with a mix of modern and antique furniture, and she always had great music playing in the background.

"I'm glad you came over, Ronnie. What happened?" Natasha's clear blue eyes anxiously searched Veronique's face. "You were crying so hard I couldn't understand what you were saying."

Natasha's velvety voice was like a salve on Veronique's frayed feelings. Anyone who heard her speak knew without a doubt that her singing voice had to be extraordinary, and it was. She was a born nurturer, always wanting to make others feel good, especially through her performances. Onstage, she was dazzling, captivating the audience to forget the daily grind and be swept away.

Veronique wiped her eyes and sighed heavily. "Sorry about that. I've been on the worst crying jag since I got here...because of Slinky. Thanks for putting me up tonight. I packed up her stuff in a box, but every time I looked around, I could see her in all her favorite places and...and I just lost it."

Natasha pushed her long, strawberry blond tresses from her face with shaky hands. "I feel horrible about Slinky. I'm worried it could have been connected to Tony, the guy I've been dating."

"Why on earth would you think that?" Veronique asked, mystified.

She swallowed a shuddering breath. "When I told him that Slinky had been killed, he got agitated and acted weird."

"Why do you think he was acting that way?"

"I don't know. He wouldn't tell me, but he was freaked out."

"What does he do for a living?"

"He owns a nightclub."

"Want me to check him out? I can do some investigating."

"No, thanks. I'm planning to break up with him. I've been trying to, but he's got a quick temper and–"

"Don't let him intimidate you, Tash. If you want, I'll go with you."

"Thanks, Ronnie, but don't worry. I can handle him," she said, her normally porcelain complexion glowing pink. "You don't have to fight everyone's battle, you know." She paused and touched Veronique's hand gently. "I saw what happened on the news this morning...about Nick. What's going on?"

By the time Veronique finished telling her everything, Natasha's eyes were huge and her mouth was hanging open. "Oh. My. God," she finally said. "I knew you had a huge crush on him at camp, but I had no idea it would carry into your adult life."

"Yeah, and I fell hard this time. I've never been in love. You know that. But from the moment I saw him again, I knew I had to have him. The passion between us was stronger than Hurricane Abby."

"Wait a minute. You two *slept* together?" Natasha said breathlessly.

"Yes. I even told him I loved him after the first time." Veronique flinched at the memory.

"You did?" Natasha's jaw dropped.

"You know me and my big mouth. No filter," Veronique said, rolling her eyes.

"Aw, don't be hard on yourself. That's what makes you loveable," Natasha said, hugging her.

"To you maybe, but I might have freaked Nick out. He was very sweet about it, but he never said he loved me back, even though he sure acted like it when we made love," she said shivering at the erotic memory. "I don't think I'll ever love like that again."

"I know the feeling." Natasha's eyes clouded with empathy.

"I'm sorry, Tash. I know what you went through with Ian."

"It's okay. I'm over him," Natasha said, but Veronique knew better, especially when Tash looked away and avoided her gaze. "Ian was a long time ago, and I had to move on." Their break up had been bad and years had passed since, yet the mere mention of Ian made Natasha miserable and regretful. Actress or not, she couldn't hide it.

Veronique's phone rang, but she didn't answer. "It's Nick. He's been leaving me messages."

"What does he say in them?"

"He wants me to call him back, but I don't want to talk to him," she muttered.

"Ronnie, you have to call him back. What if it's something about the case?"

She listened to his message and said, "Holy cow. He's downstairs."

Natasha's eyes lit up with excitement. "I'll tell the doorman to let him come up."

"No, I don't want to see him or talk to him. I'm texting him instead."

Veronique texted: *What do you want?*

Nick: *To come upstairs and talk to you.*

Veronique: *You can't. I'm visiting with Natasha.*

Nick: *Come downstairs then.*

She willed strength into her backbone and blinked back hot tears as she texted back furiously: *Go away. I'm spending the night here at Natasha's.*

He texted back immediately: *I'll come by at ten tomorrow to take you to the board meeting. Make sure you have the flash drive with the evidence.*

Insulted, she wrote: *I know what to bring. This was my investigation, remember?*

He texted back: *Do not move until I get there tomorrow.*

"Look what he just wrote. He is so bossy!" Veronique snapped, showing his text to Natasha.

NICK LOOKED out of the living room window facing the New York Stock Exchange and his stomach churned. It was the last thing he felt like looking at. The sordid memories of the past year returned and he knew without a doubt he'd be putting his apartment on the market soon. He had no intention of living—or working—in the financial district again. He'd spent most of the evening pacing and trying to make sense of things.

He wanted to return to Turquoise Bay and let the ocean wash away the day's events, but he knew the minute he stepped into his house, the absence of Ronnie would haunt every breath he took.

In spite of the convoluted mess her video had caused, *he loved her.*

The more he thought about it, the more he realized Fred was right. He owed Ronnie the benefit of the doubt. She wasn't devious; she was genuine and caring. Why would she betray him when she had been so loving with him? It didn't make sense. Ronnie was an excellent investigative reporter. She would dig for the truth and solve the puzzle of how the pictures and tape had been released. Then they could move on.

But how would she explain filming him in the first place?

He dozed off and slept fitfully. At six-thirty in the morning, his phone rang, jarring him awake. He answered right away when he saw it was Felipe's number.

"Felipe, why are you calling so early?" Nick said.

"Daisy has been injured," Felipe said in an agitated voice.

"Injured? What do you mean?" Nick's hand tightened on the phone.

"She's in the hospital," Felipe said. "I couldn't call you last night to tell you—"

"What happened?" Nick demanded.

"She was almost killed. A man shot at her, but the bullet meant for her heart, went through her shoulder instead," he said, his voice cracking.

Nick's blood ran cold. "When did this happen?"

"Late yesterday afternoon. Unfortunately, the gunman got away." He drew in a trembling breath and released it. "Daisy has done very bad things. I am very ashamed of my daughter."

An insidious chill crawled under Nick's skin. "What do you mean?"

"She sold your information to the press. Then she contacted your ex-wife and pretended she was Veronique. She bribed her to pay out a lot of cash."

"What!" Shockwaves snaked down his spine as he listened to Felipe's distraught voice.

"Daisy was so terrified, she confessed everything to me before the police questioned her last night."

Nick's stomach turned with self-loathing as he thought about how quickly he'd condemned Ronnie. He should have trusted her in spite of the damning evidence.

"It's my fault. I should have been a better father."

"It's not your fault. Daisy knew what she was doing."

"Yes, but she's so young and she has Manolito to care for. Please have mercy on her. She's my only child," Felipe pleaded.

"Don't worry too much. We'll talk about it tomorrow. I have to go now," Nick said and hung up, his mind roiling over the dire circumstances. Ronnie was in danger. A hit man was on the loose and Elizabeth was out for blood. Daisy was in the hospital after taking a bullet meant for Ronnie. He had to keep Ronnie safe and then find a way to make her forgive him. She was rightfully angry and hurt. Love involved forgiveness and trust. If he gained her trust again, she'd forgive him. He could only hope because he couldn't live without her.

He called Ronnie immediately and when it went to voice mail, he said, "Call me ASAP. It's urgent." Cursing with exasperation, he hung up and called Fred and arranged for him to go to the police and have them arrest Elizabeth at the board meeting.

Adrenaline pumped through his veins like turbo fuel as he rushed through his shower, got dressed like a madman and ran outside to hail a cab.

On his way to Natasha's apartment, he called Ronnie again

and this time she answered. "I just heard your message. Why are you calling this early?" she asked. "You said you'd come by at ten."

"I'm on my way now. Don't go anywhere until I get there," Nick said firmly.

"It's too late. I'm across the street from Natasha's buying bagels."

"Stay there. I'll be right over."

He hung up and told the cab driver, "Step on it."

CHAPTER 25

*V*eronique glanced at her watch. Eight o'clock. When she saw Nick pull up in a cab, she walked out of the restaurant to meet him. She watched as he told the driver to wait for them and got out of the car.

"Thank God, you're safe!" he said, his face drawn as he pulled her into his arms and held her tightly.

"What's wrong with you? Why are you acting so frantic?" She stiffened and disengaged herself from his arms.

"Your life is in danger. Daisy is in the hospital after taking a bullet meant for you."

Perplexed, she took a step backward and stared at him. "What are you talking about?"

"Elizabeth hired a hit man to kill you, but he shot Daisy thinking it was you," he said grimly, his eyes blazing.

Veronique's eyes bulged with shock. "Oh my God! When did this happen? Was she killed?"

"No, she survived and she's so freaked out, she confessed everything to Felipe."

"What did she confess?"

"She stole your camera and released your film to the news

station. Then she pretended to be you and blackmailed Elizabeth about the foundation. Yesterday, the contract killer that Elizabeth hired shot Daisy thinking it was you."

"Oh my God. I'm shocked. Horrified," she said, forcing the words through her parched throat. Her hands felt clammy and cold chills racked her body as she stared at him in disbelief.

"Fred is going to alert the police so they can arrest Elizabeth after the board meeting." Nick walked to the cab and opened the door. "Get in."

"I can't, I have to go back and get my purse. The flash drive is in there. I only came here with change in my pocket. Go on ahead. I'll catch a cab later."

"No, I'll wait for you."

"Okay." Veronique began to walk away from him on unsteady legs.

"Wait. I want to apologize. For everything," he said earnestly.

"It's too late for that," she said, feeling sick and utterly demoralized at the reason for his change of heart. He was only apologizing because he had solid proof that she hadn't sold him out.

"It's never too late," he said vehemently.

She faced him with her fists braced on her hips. "In this case it is. I had blind faith in you. I never needed evidence to believe you were innocent," she said, her voice faltering.

"You're right. I acted like an ass," Nick said, his voice heavy with regret and self-loathing.

She nodded. "From the first day I came to your house, you only believed the worst about me. And when my video hit the airwaves, you questioned my integrity and condemned me before we could even figure out what had happened," she said, a tear sliding down her cheek.

"Oh, baby, I'm sorry. Don't cry." He gently cradled the side of her face and wiped the tear away.

"Don't touch me," she said, her words barely able to escape her tear clogged throat.

His hand dropped to his side. "Give me a chance to make it up to you."

She wanted to, but he hadn't said he loved her. She loved him too much to continue if he didn't feel the same way, especially if he didn't trust her. "I can't. You'll just break my heart again and it hurts too much," she said, running away from him.

"Ronnie, come back," he called.

She hurried across the street to Natasha's building.

"I love you!" he shouted for all the onlookers to hear.

Her heart soaring, Veronique turned around. Out of nowhere, a black sedan came careening toward her. She tried to step out of the way, but it sideswiped her, knocking her to the ground.

The last thing she heard was Nick's anguished shout.

"*Ronnie!*" he yelled, catapulting forward.

HOURS LATER, Nick sat in the emergency room anxiously waiting for the nurse to bring Ronnie back from tests to check for a concussion and broken bones. Sick at heart, he kept replaying the horrible moment in his mind when Ronnie got hit by the car. He had never felt so powerless in his life...or so in love. When he saw her lying limply on the floor, he felt as if his heart had been wrenched from his body and decimated. He had ridden to the hospital beside her in the ambulance, watching over her as the paramedics checked her vital signs and put an oxygen mask over her face.

His phone buzzed, drawing him back to the present. He answered when he saw it was Fred calling. "Hey Fred. I don't have an update on Ronnie yet. I finally convinced Helene to go downstairs and get something to eat. She looked like she was going to pass out."

"Good thinking. I'm heading over as soon as I can. I wanted to fill you in on the board meeting."

Nick listened intently as Fred relayed to the details of the board meeting that had just ended.

"Good thing you sent Ronnie's flash drive by courier. It arrived just in time for the meeting. Elizabeth showed up late, and when we confronted her with the evidence, she tried to put the blame on her assistant," Fred said.

Nick snorted. "I'm not surprised."

"She started off acting aloof and superior, but by the time I finished with her, she was livid, especially when the board fired her. That's when the police arrived and arrested her for attempted murder and fraud."

"Good," Nick grunted.

"You should have seen her. She shrieked at them, asking if they knew who she was and threatening to have them fired."

"She's delusional."

"They had to forcefully restrain her just to handcuff her and she was still ranting when they led her away."

"She and Zack can rot in jail where they belong. I hope she gets the maximum sentence."

"Me too," Fred said. "Ronnie's accident wasn't a random hit and run. The police put out an APB for the driver's arrest. Everything was caught on camera."

"I didn't think it was an accident."

"Call me when you have news on Ronnie. I'm worried sick about her."

"Will do. Thanks, Fred. For everything," Nick said, hanging up.

When Ronnie was wheeled in on the gurney soon afterward, Nick's heart clenched when he saw her. Her complexion was eerily white, so different from her usual healthy glow. The right side of her face was bruised with a purple eyelid swollen shut and the top of her head was bandaged. He could only imagine how bruised—or broken—the rest of her beautiful body was.

"Is she going to be okay?" he whispered to the nurse, his heart aching over seeing Ronnie injured and helpless. *And all because of him.*

The nurse opened the chart and read it, the seconds ticking by like hours until she looked up and met his eyes. "The CAT scan showed she suffered a mild concussion. She was banged up pretty badly, it's amazing she didn't break any bones. We'll have the rest of the results in a few hours," she said cautiously. "Dr. Draver wants to keep her overnight for observation."

"Okay," Nick said quietly.

"I'm taking her to a room now."

"I'll follow you." Nick wished with all his heart he could pick Ronnie up and take her back to Starfish Island. He hated that his Ronnie, a free spirit who loved nature so much, was stuck in a sterile hospital like a wounded butterfly.

"Are you related to her?"

"No, but I'm responsible for her. I brought her to the hospital and signed her in."

When they arrived at the designated room, the nurse said, "There's a painkiller and sedative in her IV. If she needs anything or wakes up in pain, press this button." She indicated a remote control button on the monitor beside the hospital bed and left.

Nick stood beside the bed, willing Veronique to open her eyes. When she didn't, he dropped to his knees on the floor and bowed his head. He hadn't prayed since he was a little boy, when he would beg God to help them escape his monstrous father. Now he prayed for Ronnie to be well enough for him to take her home and nurse her with tender loving care.

"Please God. Make her be well," he repeated over and over again.

RONNIE'S EYELIDS fluttered as she struggled to center her vision. Her head felt fuzzy and her throat was parched. She slowly began to make out shapes in the room. It was dimly lit and a man was kneeling floor beside her bed. Disoriented, she stared at him.

"Nick?" she said groggily when his features finally came into focus. "What are you doing?"

"I was praying," he said quietly.

"Why?"

"For you to be okay. You had an accident, honey."

He was praying for her? "Am I in the hospital?" she said after processing what he'd just said.

"Yes, the doctor wants to monitor you. How do you feel?"

"Like I was hit by a car. Now I remember how I got here," she said after a weighted pause.

Nick flinched. "Want me to ask the nurse for more pain killer?"

"No, I don't want to be doped up." She stared at him as flash-backs of the accident invaded her mind. "You saved my life," she marveled. "*Thank you.* If I hadn't turned when you called out, the car would have killed me."

Nick heaved a tormented sigh. "Don't say that. You almost got killed because of me! I don't ever want to lose you. I'll never forgive myself for lashing out at you. I'm sorry I hurt you. Can you find it in your heart to forgive me?"

"Yes, but you need to hear me out first." She sighed. "First get up. You look positively tragic. No one is getting rid of me that easily."

"Good thing, cause I'd miss your sassy mouth." Nick sank into a chair beside her.

"I want to explain about the video. You deserve the truth, but oh God, it's embarrassing."

He raised an eyebrow. "Embarrassing? How?"

Veronique inhaled much-needed air into her lungs and said, "When I saw you working outside shirtless, I had to capture how hot you looked. I told you I wouldn't take more pictures, so I filmed you instead." She looked away from his searching gaze. "I didn't know how much longer I'd have with you and I wanted to keep it as a memory. For my eyes only. I swear," she said, her cheeks ablaze.

He leaned forward and gently kissed her head where it wasn't bandaged. "It's okay, I believe you, honey. I'm no longer upset about it. I'm, well… I'm flattered," he said with a lopsided grin.

She expelled a deep sigh of relief. "You're flattered and I'm mortified," she said ironically, wishing her vivid blush would fade as she searched the room. "Where's my purse? You needed the flash drive for the meeting."

"Don't worry, I sent it by courier and it got there on time."

"What happened at the meeting?"

"Elizabeth got kicked out as CEO and was promptly arrested and hauled away in handcuffs."

"Good!"

"She's in jail. And I just got a text from Fred that the hit man was caught near the Canadian border."

"Yay," she said weakly. "I'd smile, but it hurts too much." She looked around the room. "How long have I been in the hospital?"

"It's four o'clock. The ambulance brought you in around ten this morning. Do you remember anything about this morning?" he asked earnestly.

"I do. The most important thing," she said softly, her gaze tenderly roving his face.

"What's that? Did you see the hit man's face?"

"No, I meant when you shouted out that you loved me." She drew in a tremulous breath, hoping he'd say it again.

"I do love you, Ronnie. I was too damned stubborn and too blinded by past hurt to admit it."

"Really?" she whispered, deeply touched by his humble tone. Her heart expanded with happiness.

He loved her!

"Yes, really." He smiled and shook his head. "When I saw you that first day through the window doing a happy dance in the rain, it occurred to me how dull my life had been the past six months. I don't want to go back to Starfish Island alone. I want you beside me, making life beautiful. I can't live without you, baby."

Her heart nearly stopped with joy when he dropped to his knees again and she saw pure love reflected in his eyes. She held her breath and gazed into his beautiful eyes. He looked like he had something very important to say.

"I don't have a ring for you yet, but I'm giving you my heart since you've already stolen mine. Marry me, Ronnie. Make my life complete," Nick said, his voice hoarse with emotion.

She searched his tortured eyes. He looked so distressed, she could only imagine how guilty he felt over her almost getting killed. "You don't have to do it out of guilt, Nick. None of this was your fault. I know how you feel about marriage—"

"Hush, now you're making me upset," he growled. "I need you more than the air I breathe. If it weren't for those tubes you're connected to, I'd show you just how much right now."

"Oh, how I wish you would." Her heart felt close to bursting with so much love, it was almost painful.

"Don't worry, baby. I'll make up for lost time when I bring you home with me. We have a lifetime of loving ahead," Nick said, rising from the floor to deposit a tender kiss on her lips.

"A *whole* lifetime," Veronique agreed. Happy tears welled up as she gazed at the wonderful man who raided her heart many years ago and never let go.

EPILOGUE

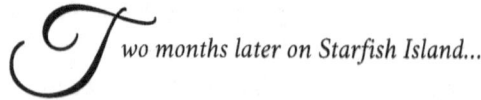*wo months later on Starfish Island...*

VERONIQUE SAT next to Nick on the porch step with her white kitten asleep on her lap. Nick had bought her the kitten when they'd returned from New York. As soon as she'd stopped bawling like a baby that he'd brought her a kitty that looked just like Slinky, she'd promptly named her Abby.

Veronique had recuperated from the accident and her bruised body was healing nicely. The doctors had voiced their amazement that she hadn't broken anything. She loved telling everyone it was hearing Nick say, "I love you," that had made her bounce, rather than break.

The past two months, Nick had watched over her like a hawk, making sure she rested and ate healthily. It was a good thing too, because she would need the extra nutrition now. Maman was in a tizzy planning her wedding and her Heart sisters had assured her they'd drop everything to be her bridesmaids. They were all rejoicing that she'd be marrying Nick.

Teddy had let out such a loud whoop that Veronique almost dropped the phone.

It seemed the happiest of all was Nick's mom, Susan. From the moment Veronique met Susan, she felt an affinity with her. A warm, affectionate woman, she'd pulled Veronique into her arms for a tight hug. When she'd stolen a moment alone with her, Susan had said, "You've made my son so happy, I love you already, Ronnie!"

Nick was happier than ever these days. The missing funds had been returned to the Cameron Hope Foundation and he was at the helm as CEO again. His next project was to fund a shelter in Miami for abused women hiding from their violent partners. Veronique was already planning a series of articles to bring awareness to their plight.

She was relieved Elizabeth was in jail awaiting trial. Vying for a lenient sentence, the hit man had pleaded guilty and confessed to killing Slinky and targeting Veronique to kill her on Elizabeth's orders.

"Look at her." Nick's voice stirred her from her musings and brought her to the present as he nodded at the tiny white kitten curled on her lap purring softly. He petted Abby's head and said, "You'd think she was attached to your lap."

"She'll have to make room for another soon," Veronique said happily.

Nick's hand went still on Abby's head as he looked up. "What do you mean?"

"Contrary to what you might think, you are not infertile, Nick Cameron," she said, grinning broadly.

"You mean?" His beautiful blue eyes searched hers with wonder.

"Yes! You're going to be a daddy."

His eyes widened as his jaw dropped. "Are you sure?"

"Yes, I'm sure," she said proudly.

"You've made me so happy!" He took Abby off her lap and set

the kitten on the floor. Lifting Veronique in his arms, he carried her inside, huskily murmuring in her ear, "I'm going to show you just how happy."

And he did until she was speechless with bliss.

For new release and giveaway parties, sign up here: http://sophiaknightly.net/newsletter-sign-up.html

Thank you for reading *Heart Raider*. If you enjoyed it, please leave a review so other readers will discover it: https://amzn.to/2FyOcDq

Turn the page to read an excerpt from *Heart Melter,* Ian and Natasha's love story. Each book in the *Heartthrob Series* is a standalone.

HEART MELTER EXCERPT

Chapter One

"You're flat," Simon called out from the third row of the dark theatre.

"No, I'm not." Natasha White gritted her teeth and raised a challenging eyebrow at the director. Her hands curved on the waist of her fawn satin teddy as she tamped down her simmering temper. Simon Worth was referring to her pitch, not her breasts, although he had spent most of the morning ogling them while she danced. It was the third time he'd rudely interrupted her song, and he'd made Freddie the choreographer change her tap number so many times, her muscles were screaming in protest. But she ignored the pain; it was worth having the starring role of Legs LaRue in "The Bee's Knees", a new roaring twenties musical sure to be a Broadway hit.

Simon was pushing hard during dress rehearsal—unfairly so. But what else could she expect from the control freak who had written the songs and lyrics of "The Bee's Knees" and was also directing it? The thirty-nine-year-old musical genius was temperamental and rude, but that wouldn't have stopped Natasha's mother, legendary Broadway diva, Anitra White, from letting loose a rant that would have singed Simon's bushy black brows. Where her acerbic mother would have screamed, Natasha held her tongue, even if she felt like strangling Simon. She didn't want any comparisons with her drama queen mama, not now, not ever.

"She was pitch perfect," her accompanist, Bruce, said instantly. Her white-haired defender pushed his horn rimmed glasses up on his high-bridged nose and glared at Simon. Bruce was an experienced, old school Broadway accompanist and nobody dared contradict him, not even Simon.

"Sounded gorgeous to me. Piss off, Simon." Freddie the chore-ographer's jaw clenched beneath his trim salt-and-pepper goatee as he sent a supportive nod Natasha's way. He had already had a meltdown this morning over Simon's intrusive meddling in his choreography. His compact dancer's body was coiled tightly, ready to spring on the director if he continued to bully Natasha. Not that she needed protecting. If she could handle her mother's tough criticism all those years growing up, she could certainly endure Simon's.

"Thanks, guys," Natasha said, blowing them kisses. She alter-nately rolled her neck and shoulders, and then peered into the theatre, her gaze zeroing in on her understudy, Lisette Raye, who watched with rabid ambition.

It was no secret Lisette was hot for the starring role—and the director. The pushy twenty-one-year-old actress and Simon were already sleeping together. Once he'd plowed through the ensemble and slept with most of them, Simon settled on Lisette, who eagerly pleased him in *all* areas. Well, she could have the pompous gasbag. Musical genius or not, he didn't appeal to Natasha, and she'd be damned if she'd sleep her way to the top. She'd seen too many failed "showmances"—mostly hook-ups that thrived during shows, but rarely made it past the last curtain call. Hanging around backstage as a child during her mom's Broadway shows had taught her to steer clear of romances in the business. It had also toughened her enough to let Simon's insults slide and not affect her performance.

"Let's take it from the top, and this time make sure your E makes me weep," Simon drawled caustically, ignoring the collective groans from Bruce and Freddie.

An hour later when Elisha, the stage manager, called lunch break, Natasha fled the theatre intent on grabbing a bite to eat and taking her Pomeranian puppy, Evita, for a quick walk. Evita was a gift from her childhood friend, Ronnie, and Ronnie's gorgeous new husband, Nick Cameron. They'd given her the puppy before leaving on their honeymoon. The moment the puppy emitted a melodious, crooning howl while Natasha sang, she promptly named her Evita, after the musical.

Natasha hurried across Times Square, her nerves frayed from Simon's heedless interruptions and unwarranted criticisms. Something wasn't right; she could feel it in her bones. Thinking back to her horoscope this morning, maybe she should heed Sydney Taggert's advice: *Keep an eye on your back and an eye toward the future.*

She zipped her tan leather jacket against the blast of ice cold air swirling around her. A bit early for such frigid weather in October, but everything this month seemed off. She usually made her way home at a brisk trot, but today her leg and butt muscles quivered from the morning's repetitive variations of the same dance. She was used to grueling workouts, but Simon had gone overboard. It was almost as if he were trying to push her to the breaking point. Well, it wasn't going to happen. He had underestimated the kind of grit she had developed over the years. She wasn't about to relinquish the plum role of Legs LaRue to a greedy newbie like Lisette.

With her head bent forward and her heavy dance tote slung across her chest, Natasha wove through the teeming crowd of tourists. She was two blocks away from her apartment when she felt a firm jerk on her dance bag. As she grappled to hold onto it and not lose her footing, a sharp pain sliced across her outer right thigh.

"Ouch!" She craned her neck to the side to see where the jab had come from. A quick glance at her leg made her gasp at the slash in her jeans and the long red line on her skin revealed by the gaping fabric. Within seconds blood rose to the cut's surface. With shaky hands, Natasha pulled her long knit scarf off her neck and tied it tightly around her upper thigh, forming a tourniquet to stop the bleeding.

She stepped onto the curb and frantically hailed a taxi. Within seconds, a cab drove up and she clambered inside.

"Where to?" the driver asked, turning to stare at her when she didn't answer right away.

Natasha could barely breathe, let alone speak as she stared at the driver. She swallowed and said through trembling lips, "Take me to the closest emergency clinic."

No, that wouldn't do. If she went to an emergency clinic, she'd be there all day. With Simon's foul mood and Lisette itching for her starring role, Natasha had to get back to rehearsal ASAP.

When the driver turned on 40th Street onto 6th Avenue, she remembered Ian's medical clinic was on that street. Her heart leaped at the thought of seeing her ex-fiancé again and it brought an onslaught of painful memories. Given the way they'd split up seven years ago, would he even agree to see her? At this crucial moment, who cared? She needed his expertise and who better than brilliant renowned cosmetic surgeon, Dr. Ian MacGregor, to treat her wound and not leave a disfiguring scar?

Knowing Ian, he'd take care of her too. He was a doctor first and foremost. Years ago, he'd been strong and protective of her... and they'd been passionately in love. Did she really want to go there after struggling for seven years to get him out of her heart? How would he react to her unexpected visit? She'd soon find out, she thought, quaking inside as she made a rash decision.

When she recognized Ian's building, she told the driver, "Stop here. Please. I'm getting off." She handed him a ten dollar bill and bolted out of the cab.

Inside the building, Natasha gulped air and tried not to look at her wound as she pressed the elevator button. Thankfully, it was empty and she rode up to Ian's office alone. But the moment she entered the reception area, she panicked at the roomful of patients waiting to be seen. Summoning strength—and courage —she limped toward the counter and tried not to put too much pressure on her injured leg.

"Excuse me," she said to a gray haired woman whose narrowed gaze was fixed on the computer screen before her. "I need to see Dr. MacGregor."

"Do you have an appointment?"

"No, but it's an emergency."

"I'm sorry. Dr. MacGregor doesn't take walk-ins," the woman replied briskly. Her name tag said Carla and Natasha wondered if she was the office manager.

"But I'm hurt," Natasha said, her voice rising in anguish. She motioned to her injured leg, hoping Carla would take pity on her.

"You're bleeding! You need to go to an emergency center. Now!" Carla said with a disapproving shake of her head.

A collective gasp sounded behind her and Natasha didn't need to turn around to confirm that all attention was riveted on her, from the buzzing voices of waiting patients to the concerned faces behind the glass reception counter.

She leaned forward and clutched the counter. "I don't feel very well. Please tell Dr. MacGregor that Natasha White needs to see him. He knows me."

"I can't interrupt him while he's with a patient," Carla said firmly.

Natasha closed her eyes and drew in calming breaths. How on earth was she going to get past Ian's gatekeeper to see him? *Desperate times called for desperate measures.* She swayed on her feet and collapsed, making sure to land carefully on her uninjured side. Good thing her acting classes had included pratfalls, she thought wryly, as she lay on the floor pretending to be unconscious.

Carla rounded the corner immediately. "Good Lord! She fainted. Get Dr. MacGregor. Quick!" she yelled, patting Natasha's cheek.

Seconds later, Natasha heard a deep male voice say, "What's going on, Carla?" He reached Natasha's side in seconds. "Tasha? Oh God. What happened?"

The hairs on Natasha's arms stood on end and butterflies swarmed her belly at the sound of Ian's rich voice, resonant with a Scottish burr. She opened her eyes and slowly met his—silver-green wolf eyes densely rimmed with sooty black lashes. Her heart pounded riotously as his arresting gaze locked with hers and a familiar weakness overcame her making it hard to breathe.

Ian's sheer male force engulfed her, held her in thrall as she lay before him, almost sick with anticipation of his next move. A jumble of potent emotions blindsided her. Longing, excitement, trepidation, despair. She hadn't realized how much seeing him again would affect her and she needed a moment to pull herself together.

Natasha closed her eyes and let her body go limp again.

Muttering "bloody hell", Ian lifted her up and carried her down the hallway and into a room. She didn't dare open her eyes. *Please let him think I'm unconscious,* she thought, mortified she'd had to resort to fainting like a damsel in distress. Before Ian, of all people.

He gently deposited her on the examining table and made short work of removing her jeans with the help of a nurse named

Judy. While the nurse cleaned the wound, Ian examined it and Natasha kept her eyes closed the whole time.

"It's superficial. I'll take it from here, Judy. Please go to Mrs. Phillips in room six. I'll be there shortly."

"Yes, Doc," Judy said and hustled out of the room.

"Nobody faints for that long. Open your eyes, Tasha," Ian said in a voice laden with irony.

Tasha. Hearing Ian's pet name for her made Natasha's heart squeeze. Her lashes fluttered as she blinked at the bright lights and focused on Ian's face. He loomed above her, handsome as ever with a straight, aristocratic nose, a firm jaw and sensual lips that rivaled any Michelangelo statue. Thick dark brows formed straight slashes above narrowed crystal green eyes that raked over her with concern. Ian's vibrant wolf eyes stirred her blood and a tremor coursed through her as his steady gaze held her immobile.

"Ian." Natasha took a deep breath of the sterile air in a fruitless attempt to calm her racing heart. "I...I..." she stammered.

Ian arched one brow and stared at her meaningfully.

She rubbed her arms against the shivery sensations he aroused, fervently hoping he couldn't tell how unhinged she felt. She stared back, trapped in his penetrating gaze. For the life of her, she couldn't think of anything to say. He had to be wondering if she'd lost her marbles.

"I'm sorry I passed out and bled all over your carpet out there. I'll have it replaced," she finally managed to say. She held her breath and waited for Ian to do something. A smile, a frown—anything to break the crackling tension between them.

Ian's mouth tightened. "I don't care about the bloody carpet. Let's turn you on your left side so I can tend to the cut." He placed a supporting hand on Natasha's upper back and carefully eased her onto her side.

The moment his warm skin touched hers, gooseflesh spread on Natasha's sensitized skin and zips of excitement shot to her pleasure points. It had always been like this with him. Ian's touch or a look from his heated eyes was all it took to set her aflame.

She huffed for air before meeting his gaze. "I probably shouldn't have come here, but I don't trust anyone else with my legs. You're the best." The moment the words left her lips, she regretted it. Where was her filter for God's sake?

Ian raised a sardonic brow. "Oh?"

This was no time for modesty, but she couldn't help feeling utterly exposed in nothing but her blouse and bikini panties. A light blanket was draped over her hip, but her legs were bare to his gaze from thigh to ankle. He kept a blank expression, professional as a doctor should, but still…

She gave a shaky laugh. "Wait, that didn't come out right. I meant you're the best physician." She cleared her throat and looked at her thigh. "Is the cut very deep? How bad is it?"

"It's not deep at all. You're lucky your jeans were in the way or it would have been worse." Ian's angular jaw was set in taut lines and his clipped tone spoke volumes.

Natasha lifted her eyes to meet his steady gaze. She was still reeling from his touch and the electrifying moment their eyes had met after so many years. Now the sexy sound of his Scottish burr and his nearness were making her heart pound and her senses buzz. This wouldn't do. Ian's intense gaze wreaked havoc on her composure as she wondered what lurked beneath the stillness.

She shivered inwardly, dropping her gaze to compose herself. He could read her like a book and he wouldn't tolerate any artifice or acting on her part. He knew her too well.

"Are you going to stitch it up?" she asked, finding her voice.

"No. I'll close the wound with tissue glue. It should heal without a scar."

"No scar? Oh good." She heaved a sigh of relief. No stitches and no scar. Now if she could just get him to smile, she'd feel a lot better.

"Be sure to keep the area clean and dry for 24 hours."

"I will. Thanks, I appreciate it." Ian's expression didn't soften when she smiled at him. With a sigh, she stared at the unyielding set of his mouth. The same mouth that had once smiled at her with heart-melting tenderness, had crooned Scottish endearments while making love to her, had kissed her *everywhere* into quivering acquiescence. All of it had been wonderful until seven years ago when she'd broken off their engagement and he'd thundered, *"Stay out of my life!"*

"How did you get cut like that?" he asked, jarring her from her musings.

"I don't know. One minute I was rushing home on my lunch break, and the next I felt a tug on my dance bag. When I pulled back, something sharp sliced across my thigh."

He touched her leg again and she jerked in response.

"Hold still," he said firmly. One masterful hand held her thigh immobile as the other treated the cut. "Are you in pain?"

"A bit."

He slanted a sympathetic look her way. "I'm almost done. I'll give you something for the pain before you leave if you still need it."

Natasha nodded and bit her lip. It wasn't so much the pain that was jolting; his touch was making her heart race and awakening every nerve portal of her body. She closed her eyes and cast aside the thrilling memory of his hands caressing her legs when they'd first made love. *Think of him as a doctor, nothing more.*

When he finished tending the wound, he straightened and folded his arms over his chest. "When was the last time you ate?" His keen eyes bored into hers.

"I had breakfast this morning. Why do you ask?" She drew aside the light blanket to inspect the large bandage wrapped around her thigh

He studied her with thoughtful deliberation. "You passed out earlier and you're thinner than I remember. Have you been on some crazy diet?"

"No, of course not," she said, wincing as she sat up. "It's all the dancing I've been doing." She wasn't about to divulge that Simon had rudely told her, "Better not lose those round tits and ass, babe. The role calls for it."

Ian's dark brows furrowed. "You used to love food." His elegant surgeon's hand turned her face toward him and his eyes settled on hers with the familiarity born of intimacy. Their eyes locked like lovers, electrified by the memory of their ill-fated passion years ago when his mere touch could set her on fire. The feel of his long fingers gently touching her face made Natasha's heart hurt. His unswerving gaze was fathomless as he stared at her.

"I still do." She drew in a heavy sigh and broke eye contact as she struggled to tether unraveling emotions. Did he remember how amazing it had been between them? Even in his sterile office, and despite the sharp headache budding behind her eyes, Ian aroused turbulent emotions inside her. She felt hot and cold and shaky at once reliving the memory of their heartbreaking split. He'd been her first and only love. No man she'd dated since had filled his shoes...or captured her heart. Especially not the last guy she'd dated. Tony Martin had been the exact opposite of Ian. Try as she might to forget Ian by dating Tony, it hadn't worked—especially when Tony revealed his violent personality. After he unleashed his nasty temper on her, she ended things right away.

Natasha's phone beeped with a text message bringing her back to her present predicament. On the way to Ian's office, between panicking and fighting nausea, she'd texted the stage manager and alerted Elisha that she'd had a minor accident and would be late.

"Will I be able to dance tomorrow?" she asked, fighting the urge to check the text.

"No. Not for several days."

"Several days?" Her shoulders slumped in spite of her resolve to be strong.

He frowned. "Do you want the wound to open again?"

"No, but..." How could she tell him this show was crucial to her career, when it was her career that had been the catalyst of their break-up?

"Follow my directions and you'll be as good as new. When was your last tetanus shot?"

Natasha shrugged. "A long time ago. Just before summer camp." A vision of Simon's snarling face suddenly made her frantic to leave. She swung her legs over the side. "I have to get back to rehearsal."

"You're not leaving until you get a tetanus shot. And you're not going to rehearsal today." Ian's steely eyes brooked no arguments. He was annoyingly authoritarian, yet a brilliant physician and a born healer. She had a scrapbook filled with newspaper and magazine articles about Dr. Ian MacGregor, the eminent laser surgeon and dermatologist, who worked magic removing disfiguring scars and birthmarks. His recent laser invention had catapulted him into celebrity status and garnered him billions.

But it was his work with underprivileged children and adults that made Natasha's heart swell with pride. Since she'd last seen him, he had traveled extensively with Doctors Without Borders and The Smile Train, removing the stigma of disfiguring cleft palates and port wine birthmarks for those who couldn't afford it. Ian would insist on not letting her leave until he could "fix" whatever was wrong with her, but she couldn't stay a moment longer.

"I don't want a shot. I have to leave now!" Not going to rehearsal was out of the question.

Ian's silver-green eyes darkened to gun metal grey as they zeroed in on her with such ferocity she fought the urge to squirm. "What in bloody hell is going on, Tasha?"

She lifted her chin. "I'm starring in a new show and we start previews tomorrow. If I don't get back to dress rehearsal, I'm going to get fined, and possibly replaced."

Ian's lip curled as he shook his head. "Nothing has changed. The show must go on. Comes before everything. Right, Tasha?"

His ironic tone irked the hell out of her. "Yes, that's right. Just like your patients always come first," she retorted. His accusation rubbed a raw spot as they faced an impasse. He was right. Nothing had changed—he was as stubborn and narrow-minded as ever when it came to her.

Natasha inched toward the edge, ready to get off the table, when his hand clamped down on her shoulder.

"Don't get up. Tetanus shot first," he said, turning to the table beside her.

She twisted her neck to see if the syringe was there, but she couldn't see over his broad shoulders. "Fine, I'll take the shot. In my arm and from someone other than you."

"I wasn't planning on it," he said coolly. "Judy will be in shortly." He turned and stalked away.

Natasha got off the examining table when he shut the door. She promptly called her agent, Marty Cranshaw, only to get the bad news that Simon had replaced her temporarily and called a put-in rehearsal for Lisette.

"No sense in going to the theatre now. Most likely they'll be there all night. Go home and rest, hon," Marty said in a caring voice.

"I will, but make no mistake, Marty. I'll be back on that stage stronger than ever for opening night," she said fervently.

Marty chuckled. "I know you will. Have I ever doubted you?"

"Nope, and that's why I love you. Bye, Marty," Natasha said, hanging up with a smile.

A smiling, middle-aged woman walked in holding a pair of blue scrubs in one hand and a small metal tray with a syringe in the other hand. "I brought these pants for you to put on after I give you the shot. We keep a few extra pairs in the office for the nurses."

"Thanks. That's very kind of you. I can't exactly leave here in a leather jacket and panties," Natasha said grimacing. "Which arm do you want? Right or left?"

"Neither. Doc ordered it in your gluteus muscle. Bottoms up," Judy said cheerfully.

"Great." Natasha rolled her eyes and privately cursed Ian. "Let's get it over with then."

"First a tiny jab, then a bit of stinging as the liquid goes in. Relax your muscles so it won't hurt," Nurse Judy said. She pulled on plastic gloves and lowered the edge of Natasha's panties, rubbing alcohol on the spot she'd inject.

Natasha gritted her teeth and silently endured the needle even though it hurt when the liquid went in.

"Okay, we're finished, dear. If the area gets sore or swollen, put an ice pack or a bag of frozen veggies on it. That should take care of it," Judy said reassuringly.

With a nod, Natasha turned over and reached for the scrubs.

"I love your hair color. I want to dye mine the same shade of red, but yours looks natural," Judy said, patting her short curly brown hair.

"It is." Natasha smiled. "You should go for it. It would look great on you."

Judy grinned broadly. "Thanks, I think I will. You're the Broadway actress aren't you?" she asked as she helped Natasha into the drawstring pants.

"Yes. Do you like musicals?"

Judy's big brown eyes sparkled with enthusiasm. "I *love* musicals. They're my biggest indulgence. I heard you're starring in 'The Bee's Knees'. When is it—"

A few sharp raps on the door interrupted her question as Ian entered. "All done?"

"Yes. All done, doc." Judy winked at Natasha and left the room.

"Are you planning any more surprise jabs before you let me go?" Natasha inquired with a sleek lift of one brow.

Ian's lips twitched. "You needed the shot, so don't complain. You can leave now, but you'll have a hard time finding a taxi at this hour. My car service will take you home."

"Thanks, that's kind of you," she said, grateful for his consideration.

"Are you still in pain?"

Natasha gave a half-shrug. "Not too much. I'll take a painkiller when I get home if it feels worse."

He handed her two prescriptions and written instructions. "Come back in a week for a recheck. I'm leaving for London tomorrow. Carla will give you an appointment with my partner, Dr. Delacorte."

Natasha hid her disappointment. He didn't intend to see her again? Ian was acting so detached, it made her nostalgic for the Ian of before—the young man who'd told her she was his first love, his only love. If he hadn't been so dead set on making her leave everything behind to join him in Scotland, things would have worked out between them. It was ironic he was still in town. *All that time wasted apart.* He had been too damn proud and stubborn to take her calls afterward, making her withdraw and immerse herself full force in her career to heal the pain of their split.

"Tell me something," she said, on impulse. "Why are you still living in New York when you were so eager to make Scotland your permanent home?"

A flash of annoyance hardened his features. "I intend to move back as soon as my clinic is ready. It's taken longer than I'd planned," he said in a strained voice.

"Oh. I'm sorry to hear it," she said softly. Natasha recalled his Aunt Maggie, whom she'd stayed in touch with over the years, telling her that Ian's inheritance was still unresolved. Was it because of that? *Better not go there.* The shuttered look on Ian's face silenced further questions.

Ian's eyes narrowed on Natasha. She might sound concerned and have a kind heart, but there was no room in it for him. Her fair cheeks glowed pink and her wide blue eyes were clouded with disappointment, yet he felt no compunction to feed her curiosity. Not now, especially when reclaiming Glenhaven was so close at hand.

The first time he'd set eyes on Natasha was when she'd visited from the States with her parents. She was a dreamy-eyed dazzler, recently graduated from Juilliard and ripe for romance. Ian's father, Malcolm, and her father, Walter, had known each other since they were students at Oxford, but it was the first time Ian had met Natasha. From that moment on he couldn't get enough of her. Her warmth and sparkling wit were just what he'd needed during the lowest point of his life when he'd learned many disturbing things about his late father. Drawn into the cocoon of her beautiful heart, Ian had immediately set out to keep her in Scotland as long as he could and make her fall in love with him as rapidly, and completely, as he had with her.

She'd stayed the whole summer and captivated not only Ian, but also his Aunt Maggie and Uncle Ranald, the caretakers of Glenhaven Estate. Tasha had embraced Scotland as if she'd always lived there. He had loved sharing his homeland with her and she'd been as delighted as a kid at Disneyworld. She'd wanted to explore every castle, sample the local food and fine Scottish whiskey and meet his friends and neighbors. By the end of that glorious summer, he wanted to keep her with him forever, but they embarked on a long-distance romance for two long years, taking numerous passion-filled trips back and forth while she performed in America and he finished his doctoral degree in biomedical science. The moment he graduated, he proposed and she accepted, tears of joy flowing down her cheeks.

Sharp desire made him shift his stance as he stared at Tasha, a stunning woman now. More enticing than ever.

"If anyone can solve this, it's you, Dr. Who," Natasha said, jolting him back to the present.

Ian stiffened at hearing her nickname for him and the teasing intonation in her voice.

"Don't you remember I used to call you that?" she said, a soft smile playing at her rosy lips.

"No," he lied, looking away from her tempting mouth. Of course, he remembered. Tasha had loved the popular British sci fi show since she'd first seen it.

"I think you do." The tiny dimple at the left corner of her mouth deepened seductively. It was the same dimple that had lured him to kiss her for the first time. Ian's palms grew damp while he scrutinized Natasha's face. *Still the face of an angel—a wayward one.* Her creamy complexion, flushed pink now, was framed by long, burnished copper curls. Luminous, curly-lashed blue eyes tantalized him, and her mouth, lush and pink, held his attention. It was the sweetest mouth he'd ever kissed—and the most deceptive.

I want a chance to make it on Broadway. Theatre is my life. I love you, Ian, but I would be miserable without performing. She'd said those words when she'd broken off their engagement—after telling him for months that she loved him and couldn't wait to be his wife! He had offered his love and a wonderful life complete with a castle and servants in Scotland, but she had made an immediate about-face right after her controlling mother had interfered.

Anitra had flown to Glenhaven from New York the previous day to muck things up between them. He recalled their meeting as if it were yesterday. The witch had laughed mockingly in his face as she'd spewed hateful words. *Natasha needs to spread her wings. She's destined to be a Broadway star like me. You didn't really think she'd give up her career to marry you and move to Scotland, did you? To be a country doctor's wife surrounded by sheep? My daughter adores the theatre, much more than she'll ever love you!*

Ian had barely held onto his temper and hadn't given into the urge to drag Anitra's bony behind out of his castle for good. Unfortunately, her harsh words were confirmed the next day when Natasha ended their engagement—by phone. He'd never forget the feeling of being gutted by her and he wasn't about to waste another second trying to figure her out. Impatient to end their little visit, Ian took hold of her elbow and helped her down from the table.

"Does your mother know you're injured?" he asked curtly.

"No, and I plan to keep it that way. I'm not the same girl you knew seven years ago. I've made it on my own, *without* Anitra's help."

"Still not calling her mum?" he said with a shake of his head.

"Nope. As far as Anitra's concerned, she's too young to have a thirty year old daughter," Natasha said ironically.

Ian snorted. "So that's how it is. Pity that."

"I don't want to talk about Anitra. Can't we make peace, Ian? Or are you going to continue scowling at me?"

Natasha's gaze was direct as she waited for his answer. Now that she'd brought it into the open, he couldn't summon the initial bitterness he'd felt at seeing her again. He just felt empty inside. She had once held the deepest part of his heart and soul captive and he'd loved her ardently, but they had no future together.

Ian headed toward the door and said, "Time to go, wee *nyaff*."

"Just a minute." Natasha grabbed his sleeve and faced him with fiery blue eyes as she tossed her flaming curls. "Don't call me an irritating little person!" She thrust her chin up and smiled slyly. "*Dunderheid*," she retaliated, daring to insult him.

Ian stifled the rumble of caustic laughter rising in his chest.

They hadn't spent more than an hour together and they were already trading insults. Tasha had a way of getting under his skin and provoking him more than anyone else could, yet her quick wit never ceased to entertain him.

Striding out the door, he squashed the powerful urge to turn and grab the maddening redhead and kiss her senseless. And that wasn't all he felt like doing.

Click to keep reading HEART MELTER: https://amzn.to/348BmGj

TROPICAL HEAT SERIES - Each book is a standalone.

Wooed by You - Linc and Isabel

Wild for You - Clay and Marisol

Sold on You - Marcos and Gabriela

Kissed by You - Alex and Georgina

Loved by You - Roman and Piper

HEARTTHROB SERIES - Each book is a standalone.

Heart Raider - Nick and Veronique

Heart Melter - Ian and Natasha

Heart Tamer - Alec and Kate

Heart Hunter - Cameron and Evie

Heart Tempter - Leo and Teddy

Heart Stealer - Stone and Ivy

FALCONS IN LOVE - Each book is a standalone.

Scent of Love

The Holiday Sweet Spot

BEACH READ SERIES - Each book is a standalone.

Grill Me, Baby

Blame it on Romeo

ABOUT SOPHIA KNIGHTLY

New York Times & USA Today bestselling author, Sophia Knightly cooks up hot romance and delicious humor in her sexy contemporary romances that pair hot, alpha heroes with strong, smart women and throw them on a challenging emotional journey. Published by St. Martin's Press, Kensington, and Samhain Publishing, her popular *Tropical Heat Series* and *Heartthrob Series* have consistently been on multiple best selling lists.

Sophia loves writing books that end with a sigh and a smile. In addition to traveling, foodie adventures, and enjoying the arts in all forms, one of her favorite pastimes is simply watching people--especially those in love!

Sign up for Sophia's Book News and Giveaways at:
http://sophiaknightly.net/newsletter-sign-up.html

Subscribe to Sophia's YouTube Channel :
http://bit.ly/2oKY8A3

Visit Sophia's Website:
sophiaknightly.net
Write to Sophia:
sophiaknightly@gmail.com